Been

Adrienne Thompson

Pink Cashmere Publishing Co.

USA

Edited by: Alyndria Mooney with Jessica Meigs

Cover Design by: Adrienne Thompson

This is a work of fiction. Names, characters, businesses, places,
events and incidents are either the products of the author's
imagination or used in a fictitious manner. Any resemblance
to actual persons, living or dead, or actual events is purely
coincidental.

Printed in the United States of America

First Printing 2012

ISBN: 0983756929

ISBN-13: 978-0983756927

Also by Adrienne Thompson

*BLUES*DAY

Praise for *Bluesday* by Adrienne Thompson:

"...I highly recommend this book to anyone that wants to read a book that has a believable storyline and characters..."
-OOSA Online Book Club (5 stars)

"Thompson delivered a very realistic story of a woman who has buried secrets deep within her heart."
-APOOO Book Club (4 stars)

Acknowledgements

Dear Lord, You are my everything. Thank you for blessing me, despite my faults.

To my children, Alyndria, Rickey Jr., and Adrienne II, who have always been my greatest inspiration, I pray that I have been half as good to you as you have been to me. I love you, and you have made me the proudest mother in the world!

A special thank you to Orsayor Simmons, Angela Remley, the lovely ladies of the Divas Leaving No Pages Unturned Bookclub (Toshona Carter, TaCarla Young, Channon Horne, Shereen Watkins, Cassandra Wallace, Angela Davis, Tanya Davis, LaToshia Enoch, Shantwan Vickers, Tineal Williams, Rosalyn Barnes, Jennifer James, Donna Barnes, and Sherrie Phillips), Margie Nesby, Sandra Branscomb, LeAndria Tartt, Marilyn Foster, Esther Cope, Alicia Smith-Perdue, Camesha Williams-White, Tonya Mazora, Twana Davis-Williams, Mary Johnson, Willie Carmickle, Repunza Brown, Linda Williams-Ross, Julia Press Simmons, and my family and friends for all of your support! God bless you and I love you all!

In loving memory of my friend, Nancy Moore. Rest in peace.

Love bears all things, believes all things, hopes all things, endures all things.

1 Corinthians 13:7 ESV

Soundtrack provided by Ms. Anita Baker

"Fairy Tales"

"Sometimes I Wonder Why"

"Rules"

"Serious"

"Whatever It Takes"

"I Apologize"

"How Does it Feel?"

"You're My Everything"

"Men in My Life"

"Talk to Me"

"Mystery"

"Giving You the Best That I Got"

"Plenty of Room"

"Body and Soul"

"Been So Long"

"It's Been You"

"You Belong To Me"

"Ain't No Need to Worry"

"I Can't Sleep"

"Angel"

"Only For a While"

"No More Tears"

"Same Ole Love"

Prologue

I sat in the corner of the student union, laughing it up with my friend, Brenda. Brenda was a cool, junior Poly Sci major. I was a freshman, but I played the role of an upperclassman pretty well. The only ones who knew I was a freshman were the people in my classes and Corey, since we came here together. I was waiting for Corey that day. We were going to dinner together and then up to his room to study. No hanky panky. Corey was too good a guy for that. Well, maybe not even that. Maybe he was just too focused. His father was a military man. Discipline and focus had been taught to Corey from the time he was born. He was at the U of A for one reason: a degree. I was just along for the ride. Or at least that's how it seemed. When he wasn't in class or studying, he was doing work study or practicing with the basketball team or the baseball team or volunteering. That's why he was late that day. Obligations. That's why I was sitting in the union with Brenda, and that's how I met Wasif.

When Wasif Masood walked into the room, he may as well have had a spotlight following him. He was all I saw from that point on.

He stood 5'10" tall. He was slim with flawless, tanned skin. At that moment, I thought maybe he was Arabian or Indian. I wasn't sure, but his features told me he was of Middle Eastern decent. His cold black hair was thick and wavy. He was wearing a university hoodie and jogging pants. He was smiling brightly, yucking it up with a couple of guys, one black and the other white. He had the most beautiful smile.

"Hey, guys," Brenda said. I'd forgotten that Brenda was even there.

The black guy said, "Yo, what's up, Bren?"

Wasif looked in my direction, and our eyes locked. I swear electricity sparked between us. After that day, I forgot I was in college for a degree in library science. I forgot Corey was my boyfriend. I forgot everything and everyone except Wasif Masood…

Chapter 1

"Fairy Tales"

I hate my name. Always have. Mona-Lisa Dandridge. What kind of name is that? Oh, I know that the Mona Lisa is a famous work of art. I know that Leonardo DaVinci was one of the greats, a genius really. Maybe I should be honored to have the name, but I'm not. Maybe it would've been better if Mona was my first name and Lisa was my middle name. But no, Mona-Lisa is one name, hyphenated. My middle name is DaVinci. Yeah, you heard me right, Mona-Lisa DaVinci Dandridge. My name is concrete proof that sixteen-year-old girls shouldn't have babies — or at least they shouldn't be allowed to name them. There are other reasons why a girl that young shouldn't have kids, but I won't go into them right now.

Anyway, I used to wonder why my mom didn't just give me her name. Christina is a pretty name. I could've dealt with that. But no, I got stuck with a stripper's name. Maybe if my father had stuck around long enough for me to be born, he would've stepped in and given me a normal name like Tasha or Andrea. But he disappeared as soon as the plus sign showed up in the window of the home pregnancy test. Mama said his name was Michael Tolliver. I met him once, I think. Well, that's a long story. One I've tried not to remember.

Anyway, Michael's a nice name. Maybe he would've named me Michelle. That would've been nice. Michelle Dandridge has a nice ring to it. Oh well, I've been Mona-Lisa Dandridge for thirty-three years now. I may as well accept it. At least my name isn't Cleopatra, like my younger sister. Cleopatra Egypt Williams. I guess twenty is not a good age for motherhood either, if you use my mother as an example. My mother loved to read, and she loved art and history, but I think that she may have misused her knowledge.

I shook my head, trying to shake my own thoughts loose, as I pulled my Chrysler Pacifica to a stop in front of the junior high school and unlocked the doors.

"Bye, Mama," my sons said in unison as they jumped out of the truck.

"Bye, boys. Have a great day," I called after them. But by then, they were already halfway across the yard, on their way to the double entry doors. I sighed. They were growing up so fast. It seemed like just yesterday their father and I were changing their diapers and fixing formula. Now they'd both outgrown my 5'6" and were in the ninth grade. Morgan was even beginning to grow facial hair! That made my mind go tilt for real. What was I going to do when my boys were all grown up?

Morgan and Blair. I'd named my twin sons after my two favorite actors. They were fraternal twins and best friends. Morgan was just a hair taller than Blair. Blair was almost a carbon copy of their father, barely resembling me at all. He was Wasif all over again, from his brown eyes, to his keen nose, right down to his dark olive skin and thick wavy black hair. Morgan took after my side of the family for the most part. He had my hazel eyes and fine curly hair. He even had my ears and full mouth. His nose was a little larger than mine. His skin was a shade lighter than my medium brown. They'd both inherited their father's tall, lanky build.

I headed back to our house on Scherman Oaks Circle. I had plenty to do before the school day ended and no time to waste. I had to make sure the house was spotless before Wasif made it home. Wasif was a neat freak, and since I didn't work, he would throw a fit if he came home to messy house. I had to pick up some dry cleaning, take the dog to the groomers, and then fix dinner. I definitely had a busy day ahead of me.

♦♦♦

The day zipped by, as all busy days do, and before I knew it, Wasif had arrived. "Your dad's home!" I yelled from the kitchen. The boys were in the living room playing a video game. I'd just heard the garage door open.

"We hear him!" Blair said excitedly.

I pulled the baked chicken from the oven and laid the pan on the counter. I turned around to find Wasif standing in the kitchen doorway holding a bouquet of yellow roses. "Hello, beautiful," he said. Wasif's beauty far outshined that of the roses he held. With chiseled features and a gorgeous white smile, he was perfection.

I walked over to him and planted a long kiss on his lips. "Hey, baby. For me?" I pointed to the roses.

"No, they're for Lizzie," he said with a wide smile.

"Well, Lizzie's already enjoyed a trip to the groomer's, so I'll take the flowers."

He shrugged. "That's between you and Lizzie."

I rolled my eyes and turned back to the counter. Wasif

grabbed me from behind and kissed the back of my neck. "You know they're for you. How was your day?"

I turned around and hugged him. "Busy. How was yours?"

"Tiring. Three bypasses today. *Three*. I'll be dreaming about hearts and arteries tonight for sure."

I kissed his cheek. "Mmhmm. I guess I'll have to work extra hard to put something else on your mind then, huh?"

He smiled down at me and stroked my cheek with his finger. "You know just what to do, don't you, babe?"

I nodded. "Always. Did you miss me?"

He leaned in and planted a slow kiss on my lips. "What do you think?"

"Mm, I missed you, too."

After dinner, Wasif and the boys played video games for a while. I smiled as I watched him interact with them. Wasif was a great father, and it made me feel so good that my boys had him in their lives. Like I said before, I'd only met my father once in my entire life, and it wasn't under the best of circumstances. I'd always been determined for my children to have better, and I'd succeeded. I was proud of my family.

I announced bedtime at 9:30, and the boys grumbled all the way to their rooms. I sat down on the sofa next to Wasif and laid my head on his shoulder. "I love you so much, Wasif."

"I love you too, babe. More than you'll ever know."

We sat there for a few more minutes, enjoying each other's company, and then he stood from the couch and reached for my hand. "Come with me, pretty babe."

I smiled and took his hand. He led me to our bedroom where he showed me exactly how much he loved me over and over again. The next morning, when he left for work, I felt that familiar pain in my heart that I always felt on Tuesday mornings. It would be a week before I saw him again. He was going home to his wife that evening.

Chapter 2

"Sometimes I Wonder Why"

Along with that pain in my heart, I woke up that morning with an odd feeling, a feeling that I'd never experienced before. It was almost as if I felt bad about our situation. As if my conscience was picking at me. I wondered if that voice was going to pop back into my head again. The one that used to tell me that what I was doing with Wasif was wrong. I'd silenced it long ago. It was the only way I'd been able to hold my life together.

I opened my eyes and looked around the bedroom. The flowers that Wasif had brought me were in a vase on the dresser. Streams of light snuck in through the slats of the mini blinds, forming a pattern of lines on the wall. I rolled over and looked at Wasif's side of the bed, his *empty* side of the bed. There was still a dent in his pillow, and I could still smell his natural scent on the sheets. I took a deep breath and sighed.

Ok, I can admit that I felt a little lonely. Ok…maybe *more* than a little. One day a week with the man I love wasn't exactly ideal, but it was what it was, and I had accepted it. I loved him, and I knew that he loved me, but his marriage had been arranged long before the two of us ever met. Wasif respected his parents and would do anything to please his father. It had hurt when he married his wife, but I understood why he felt he had to do it.

I sat up on the side of the bed and stretched. I stood and inspected my body in the dresser mirror. I rubbed my hand across my fleshy stomach, the remnants of having carried twins fourteen years earlier. Along with my stomach came additional flesh to my hips and backside, but Wasif never complained. He seemed to love every inch of me.

I told myself that I needed to get a move on. I'd have to get the boys up soon for school. After I dropped them off, I'd spend the day doing what I usually did, reading or watching TV. I showered and dressed, cooked a light breakfast, and then coaxed my boys out of bed. I watched as they drug themselves to the kitchen table. My boys are beautiful, brown princes. A perfect combination of two different worlds, just like their father and mother. I smiled. As odd as our situation was, my boys made me feel it was all worthwhile.

Loaded down with heavy backpacks, Blair and Morgan climbed into the truck. Both sat in the backseat, an arrangement made to eliminate daily fights over who sat in the front seat. They were very close yet still very competitive. Morgan teased Blair about being taller than him. Blair teased Morgan because his grades were better. But, if anyone tried to come between them, they'd fiercely defend one another. They were good boys, and I was more than proud of them.

They hopped out of the truck in front of the school and disappeared into the bustling crowd of pubescence and hormones. I sighed, turned my vehicle around, and headed home the long way. By the long way, I mean I took a detour out of town to Little Rock. The weather was nice for October, so why not take a little drive? Then again, weather in Arkansas was unpredictable at best. It was sixty degrees, but by noon, it might've dropped to forty. I took I-40 and quickly drove the twenty-seven miles from Conway to Little Rock, then took the expressway to Chenal Parkway.

In Little Rock, I slowed as I passed the office of Cardiothoracic Associates of Central Arkansas. It was the office that Dr. Wasif Masood shared with Dr. Fahad Masood, his father. Both were successful cardiothoracic surgeons, well respected in Arkansas. I slowed even more when I saw

Wasif's shiny midnight blue Range Rover. I ached a little. I wished I could walk in there and surprise him. I wished I was his wife. But I wasn't his wife and wishing was a waste of time.

The blaring of car horns behind me snapped me out of my thoughts and made me realize that I'd come to a complete stop and was blocking traffic. I don't know why, but I hit my turn signal and pulled into the parking lot at Wasif's office. Maybe I just felt bold or maybe I'd lost my mind, but for whatever reason, I found myself parking in front of the office. I pulled on a pair of Fendi sunglasses, grabbed my Gucci purse, and headed into the office.

I smiled as I walked through the nearly packed waiting area and approached the receptionist's window. A blond-headed young lady returned my smile and said, "Can I help you?" Her southern accent was thick, almost comical.

I nodded. "Yes, I don't have an appointment or anything, but I was wondering if I could see Dr. Wasif Masood. He was my mother's surgeon, and I need to ask him some questions." It was a believable lie.

"Oh, well, what's your mother's name?"

"Just tell him that Mo Dandridge needs to speak with him. He'll remember me."

She shrugged and gave me a skeptical look. "Ok, but even if he agrees to see you, it may take awhile. He has a lot of appointments this morning." *Wanna bet?*

I nodded. "I understand."

I took the only vacant seat, which was right underneath the flat-screen TV that hung on the wall, and smiled at the rainbow of patients in the waiting area. I'd only been sitting and waiting for two minutes when she told me that he was ready to see me. I hadn't even had time to flip through the magazine I'd picked up. I thanked her as she led me to his office.

"Thanks, Paula," Wasif said to the receptionist. "Ms. Dandridge, how can I help you?"

The room smelled of the familiar scent of his cologne. I waited for him to close and lock the door, and then I smiled and whispered, "I really need your help, doctor. I missed you."

With wide eyes, he said, "Mo, what in the world are you doing here? What if my father sees you here? I'll never hear the end of it."

I pointed to the huge window behind his cluttered desk. "Then you'd better close the blinds."

He nodded. "You're right." As he turned and walked to the

window, he said, "Mo, you've got to go. I'll call you later."

I looked around the office as I stepped out of my heels. Behind his huge mahogany desk sat an empty executive chair. There were framed diplomas on the ecru wall from The University of Arkansas and the University of Arkansas for Medical Sciences. I could see a picture frame lying flat on the bookcase beside me. *Probably a picture of his wife and daughters.* I laid my purse in the burgundy leather chair in front of his desk, and when he turned back around, I'd stripped out of my skinny jeans and blouse and was wearing nothing but my matching pink underwear. I tilted my head to the side and gave him an innocent look. "I should go?"

He bucked his eyes as I slowly walked towards him. "Um...Mo..."

I sat on top of the desk without bothering to move any of the papers. I grabbed his hand and pulled him closer to me. He smiled. "W...what are you doing, babe?"

I kissed him softly. "I told you. I missed you, doctor," I whined.

He nodded as I loosened his tie, unbuttoned his collar, and kissed his neck. "Uh...I missed you, too, but y...you can't just show up like this, babe."

I shrugged. "Ok, doctor. I'll go then." I tried to slide off of his desk, but he blocked me.

He leaned over and kissed me as he pulled his dress shirt out of his pants. "No, Ms. Dandridge. First, you've got to finish what you've started."

"What about your patients, Dr. Masood?"

He smiled as he laid me back on his desk. "They can wait. This is an emergency."

Thirty minutes later, I emerged from the office with a satisfied glow and smiled as I passed the patients in the reception area. *Now, that's enough to get me through the week.* I loved Wasif with all of my heart, and I'd never been unfaithful to him. I'd wait a year for another visit if I had to, but I knew that Wasif couldn't. He loved and needed me, and I must say that it felt good to know that. It felt good to be his woman, even if it was only for one day a week.

I turned the radio up and let the sounds of an old Anita Baker song fill my vehicle as I coasted down Interstate 40, headed back to Conway. I was halfway home when my cell phone rang. "Hello?"

"You are a very mean woman," Wasif said softly into the phone.

I smiled. "Now, why would you say that?"

"Because now I have a job to do, and all I can think about is you, your body, your scent. I wish I could've shut this place down and spent the entire day making love to you. I miss you already."

"Mmm, that would've been nice. We'll have to do that one day. Spend the whole day in each other's arms, like we used to. Remember?"

"I remember back then I couldn't get enough of you. I still can't. I love you, babe."

"I love you, too. Get back to work, Dr. Masood."

"I will. Talk to you later. Bye, babe."

"Bye."

I smiled all the way home.

The rest of that day went by pretty slowly. Time always seemed to slow down when Wasif was gone. It always seemed that it took a million years for Monday to roll back around. I spent that day reading and watching TV. I was glad when it was time to pick up the boys. I hated being alone more than anything in the world.

I pulled my car up to the school and smiled as I spotted my boys. Morgan was talking to a girl and Blair was standing next to him. A girl! Wow, they were really growing up too fast.

Soon they'd have girlfriends and want to go out on dates. I shook my head. *How am I gonna deal with this stuff?*

I hit the button to unlock the doors and watched as they finally approached the car. Once they'd climbed inside, I said, "You guys have a good day today?"

"Yep," Morgan said.

"It was ok," was Blair's slow response.

I raised my eyebrows as I began to pull off the lot. "Just ok?"

I looked in the rearview mirror to see Blair shrug his answer. I sighed and decided to leave him alone for that moment. I'd just try to talk to him later.

Back at home, we had chicken fried steak, mashed potatoes and gravy, and English peas for dinner. Afterwards, the boys headed to their rooms to finish their homework, and I headed to my room to wait for my nightly phone call. Like clockwork, my phone rang at nine o'clock. It was Wasif.

I answered it with, "Hey, handsome."

I could hear him smiling through the phone. "Hello, beautiful. How was the rest of your day?"

I lay back in the bed. "Lonely without you. I miss you."

"Yeah, I definitely miss you, too. Wish I was there," he said softly.

"And what would you do if you were here?"

"You really want to know?"

"Mmhmm."

"Well, first I'd…"

The conversation went on for an hour and by the time we were done, I was almost satisfied again. *Almost.* I couldn't wait for the next Monday. Yeah, I loved me some Wasif Masood.

◆◆◆

Early the next morning, I walked into Blair's room and gently shook him awake. "Blair, wake up, sweetheart. I need to talk to you."

With drowsy eyes that mirrored his father's, he looked up at me. "Ma'am?"

I sat down on the side of his twin bed and took his hand in mine. "What's going on at school?"

He closed his eyes and scratched his forehead. "Nothing."

"Blair, something is bothering you. You can tell me."

He turned and looked at the wall beside his bed.

"Ok, if you ever want to talk about it, I'm ready to listen." I leaned over and kissed his cheek. "I love you, Blair."

"I love you, too, Mama." I left his room with heaviness in my heart. Something was bothering my baby, and I wanted to fix it. Just like any other mother, I wanted to take his pain away.

During breakfast, Morgan chatted away about the day ahead, and Blair was quiet. I was still worried about him when I dropped them off at school. Blair was still on my mind as I ran errands that morning. When I finally made it back home around 11 A.M, I told myself to stop worrying. He'd talk when he was ready to. That was just his personality. He was much quieter than Morgan, an introvert. He'd be ok.

After making my bed and washing the dishes, I settled down on the sofa with the latest installment of the Tennyson Hardwick novels. Reading had been a passion of my mother's. It was the one and only redeeming quality about her and the only one I'd inherited from her. I had only made it through one paragraph when the phone rang.

"Hello?"

"Ms. Dandridge?" said the voice on the other end.

"Yes. Who's this?"

"Ms. Dandridge, this is Ms. French, the counselor at your son's school. Can you come and meet with me? There's been a problem with your son."

I frowned. "Which one?"

"Blair."

My eyes widened. *"Really?* Ok, I'll be there shortly." Something was wrong. Blair never got in trouble. I could've believed Morgan, but not Blair. Something was definitely going on with him.

I slipped on my shoes and headed out to the school.

I stepped into the counselor's small office and saw Blair sitting in a chair next to another young man. The other boy was pale-skinned with blonde hair and green eyes. Both boys looked like they were ready to murder each other. I'd never seen that much hate and anger in Blair's face before. It disturbed me to see him like that.

"Have a seat, Ms. Dandridge," the counselor said.

I offered her a smile and then sat between the boys. I looked over at Blair, but he kept his eyes on the floor.

"While we're waiting for Sam's parents, I'll fill you in on what has happened. The boys got into a verbal argument during Algebra and ended up in a physical fight. As you know, there's a zero-tolerance policy at this school for fighting."

"I can agree with that. Zero tolerance is a good policy when it comes to violence." I looked over at Blair. "What was the argument about, son?"

With a shaky voice, Blair said, "He said I was a terrorist. Called me Blair Bin-Laden. I told him I'm half-Pakistani. Bin Laden was Arabian."

"Same difference," Sam muttered.

I frowned. "What's your policy on bullying?" I asked the counselor.

She cleared her throat. Her face was turning red, nearly matching the blazer she wore. "Zero-tolerance as well. But I'd hardly call what Sam said bullying."

Before I could reply, a woman whom I assumed was Sam's mother walked into the office and took a seat on the other side of her son. She and Sam shared the same pale skin and green eyes. She introduced herself as Kara Quimby. She was wearing baggy jeans and an oversized sweatshirt, both of which hung from her thin frame. Judging from the bags under her eyes, trouble and worry were no strangers to her. I offered her a fake smile and introduced myself and wondered what it felt like to be the mother of a racist.

Ms. French filled her in on what had transpired between the boys. "Sam, you should apologize," Ms. Quimby said in a noncommittal tone.

"No," Sam said matter-of-factly.

"Sam! Apologize!" she insisted, embarrassment written all over her face.

"No! I hate his Iraqi ass. I hate him! My dad got killed in Iraq!"

"I'm not Iraqi!" Blair yelled. "And I'm tired of you messing with me! My dad is Pakistani! *Pakistani*! *Not* Iraqi!"

Sam jumped up from his chair, and I noticed that he was shorter than Blair, but he more than made up for his height in weight. "Whatever! Your people come over here and take all the jobs! You, with your liquor stores and gas stations. You're not even a real American! I hate you! Why don't you just go back to where you came from?!" Someone had fed Sam a load of racist propaganda. I had a feeling I knew who it was.

Blair sprung to his feet. "My dad's a doctor, you idiot! He saves lives! He was born in America and so was I! That makes us both American citizens, stupid! Do your research!"

Sam balled up his fists. "You look like one of them terrorists, so that means you *are* one of them! I wish you all were dead! My dad died for nothing, you stupid rag-head!"

"Sam!" his mother shouted.

"I bet he's got a bomb in his backpack! That terrorist is gonna kill all of us!" Sam screamed, his face beet red.

"Sam! Stop this right now!" his mother said. Sam breezed past her and slammed the door behind him, rattling the counselor's many "Counselor of the Year" plaques that hung proudly on the wall. His mother gave me an apologetic look and hurriedly left the office.

Blair's face was a flushed combination of brown and red. He was breathing heavily.

"Sit down, Blair." Blair fell back into the chair and hung his head, still breathing heaving breaths. I placed my hand on his shoulder. "Calm down." He closed his eyes and nodded his head.

"What are you going to do about this?" I asked the counselor.

She looked at me with wide eyes and flipped her long, fuzzy brunette hair over her shoulder. "Well, both boys will have detention for three days, starting tomorrow morning. They will be sent home for the rest of today."

I frowned. "They have detention *together*?"

"Well, yes, but they'll be closely supervised."

"They'd better be." I stood from the chair. "Come on, Blair. Let's go."

We left, and I fought back the tears as I watched Blair climb into the front seat and fasten his seatbelt. "Blair, I know what that boy said to you upset you, but fighting is not the answer."

He turned his head and looked out the window. "I know, Mama. I tried not to fight him, but he just kept talking. I just wanted to shut him up."

"I understand that, baby. Next time, just tell a teacher or walk away. Be the bigger person, okay?"

Blair nodded.

I fought tears of frustration all the way home. It wasn't until I was inside my house and Blair had closed himself in his room that I finally let loose. I shut myself in my bedroom and cried like a baby. I didn't know what to do, but I wished that I could kick Sam's butt and his mama's too. *This is what's been bothering Blair. A boy needs his father at a time like this.* I wished that Wasif had been there to talk to Blair. I wished that I could take Blair's pain away. I wished that Sam Quimby would evaporate from the earth. There I go wishing again.

Chapter 3

"Rules"

I woke up to someone tapping me on the shoulder. I rolled over and looked at the clock. 4:00 P.M. I bolted up in the bed to see that it was Morgan standing over me. I hadn't even realized I'd fallen asleep, but then again, crying always made me sleepy. I hated to cry almost as much as I hated being alone.

I sat up on the side of the bed. "Morgan! How'd you get home?"

He silently turned towards the doorway. I followed his gaze. Standing there was an older version of Wasif. The elder Dr. Masood. He was a little shorter and much heavier than Wasif. I'd only been in the same room with him twice in the fifteen years I'd known Wasif. Today made three times. He'd always known about me and the boys, and while he didn't readily accept the situation, he was a man who believed in being responsible. Wasif had made his bed, and his father expected him to lie in it. When Wasif was still in college and medical school, it had been Dr. Masood who'd supported me and the twins financially. He was a man who demanded respect, and I always gave it to him.

"Uh, thank you, Dr. Masood. I must've drifted off without realizing it," I said nervously.

His only response was a nod, and then he turned and left. He didn't even ask to see Blair.

I looked up at Morgan. "I'm sorry. I must've left my phone in the car."

Morgan shrugged. "It's okay. I called Dad, and he had Dr. Masood pick me up." *Dr. Masood, not Grandpa.* "Is Blair alright?"

I nodded. "He's in his room. Did you see what happened?"

He shook his head. "Naw, heard about it though. That Sam dude's been messing with him for a while, calling him names, throwing pencils at him in class, tripping him. I told Blair I'd handle him, but he told me to leave it alone."

Suddenly, I understood what had led Blair to fight him. He'd reached his breaking point with that Sam boy. "Handle him? Don't you be getting into any fights, Morgan. Let me and your dad handle this."

Morgan shrugged again and shoved his hands in his pockets. He cocked his head to the side and said, "Ok."

"Does this Sam ever mess with you?"

He shook his head. "Naw, I don't look like Dad, and anyway, he knows better." Morgan thought that he was tougher than he really was. Of the two, he was the most confident. Sometimes he was *overly* confident.

"No fighting, Morgan. In everything you do, you represent me and your father. Remember that."

"Then I guess he better not mess with me," Morgan said wryly.

I sighed. Raising a man was definitely no job for a woman to do alone. "Go do your homework. I need to get started on dinner."

"Yes, ma'am."

I followed him out of my room but passed the kitchen and headed to Blair's room. His door was closed, and I could hear music playing. I knocked and waited for him to answer. The music stopped, but Blair didn't come to the door.

"Blair, can I come in?"

After a moment of silence, I heard a muffled, "Yes, ma'am."

I opened the door to find Blair sitting on his bed with his back against the headboard. He'd changed from his jeans and t-shirt into a pair of basketball shorts, and his skinny chest was bare. His thin frame was so much like Wasif's that it was mind-boggling. I sat at the foot of his bed and smiled weakly. "Do you want to talk now?"

He shook his head. "Not really."

I looked across the room at the dresser. It was lined with pictures of Blair and Morgan and of both of them with Wasif.

"I was proud of you today, Blair," I said.

He looked up at me. "Why? I got in trouble."

"You shouldn't have fought him, but I was proud of the way you defended your heritage. There's nothing wrong with you, Blair. There's nothing wrong with the way you look. You know that, right?"

He shrugged. "I guess."

I reached over and rested my hand on his leg. "You are a very handsome young man, and I'm not just saying that because I'm your mother. You are beautiful. Don't you ever forget that."

He nodded. "But I'm different, Ma. I don't look like anyone at that school."

"Different is good, Blair. It's what makes you stand out. It makes you special. One day, you'll be thankful for your looks."

"If you say so. Thanks, Ma."

I stood and then leaned over and hugged him.

"Can I call Dad?" he asked.

I hesitated and then said, "When he calls tonight, I'll be sure you get to talk to him."

"Ok."

I left his room hoping that things would get better for him because honestly, I wasn't sure if I could handle much more. I hoped that Wasif's call wouldn't be a short one. Blair really needed to talk to him. He really needed his father.

We had individual night for dinner. The boys pigged out on frozen pizzas, and I had a salad and a sandwich. They were in the den playing video games when Wasif called me. I was in my bedroom.

"So my dad got Morgan home safely, huh?" Wasif said in a weary voice.

I cradled the phone between my ear and my shoulder as I painted my toenails. "Yeah, I'm really sorry about that. I guess I dozed off without realizing it. What did your father have to say?"

He paused and then said, "Nothing, really." That translated to *nothing good*.

I set the hot pink nail polish on the nightstand. "Yes, he did.

You sound upset. What did he say, Wasif?"

He sighed woefully. "Just something about me needing to get this situation under control and something else about you being irresponsible and unfit."

I frowned. "What?!" I wished he hadn't told me. I wished I hadn't asked. I wished, I wished, I wished...

"I know. I shouldn't have asked him to do it, but when Morgan called, I was in the middle of a procedure. The nurse had to answer my phone for me. I couldn't just leave my son stranded there. I tried to call you, but you didn't answer. Dad happened to be working in Conway. Who else was I supposed to ask?" He was almost whining. I could imagine he'd sounded similar when he'd called his father.

"Well, I'm really sorry, baby. I was upset about the whole thing with Blair and I cried, and you know I get sleepy when I cry. It won't happen again."

"Yeah, well, it's ok. In a couple of years, I'll get them cars. That'll help."

"Ok."

"Hey, hold on a moment, ok?"

"Sure."

I listened to Wasif have a muffed conversation in Punjabi, his family's native language. I could hear a female's voice, too.

His wife.

Wasif finally returned to the phone and whispered, "I've gotta go, babe. Love you."

"Love you, too. You wanna talk to Blair about what happened today? He wants to talk to you. He really defended you and his heritage. You would've been proud."

"I'll call him on his phone tomorrow. Bye."

"Bye."

Wasif loved his sons, and no one could convince me otherwise. He loved them, and he did the best he could by them. He took care of them better than some men who lived in the same house with their kids. My boys had the best of everything, and they wanted for nothing. Wasif Masood was a good man in an impossible situation. He had stress all around him, and I'd just made things worse for him. I vowed to make it up to him. I loved him, and you take care of the people you love, right?

Chapter 4

"Serious"

I was standing in the checkout line at the grocery store the next day remembering the look on Blair's face when I told him that Wasif would call him later. He looked so disappointed that, for the first time in a while, I started to think that maybe our arrangement was hurting the boys. Wasif wasn't as accessible to them as he should've been, but when he was around, he was so good to them. I shook my head. *Everything is fine. Blair will be ok.* I was almost to the front of the line when my cell phone rang. It was the school again. *Damn!* I thought. *What now?* "Hello?"

"Ms. Dandridge?"

"Yes?"

"This is Ms. French, from the school?" she said as if she was questioning her own identity. "Um, can you come and meet with me again?"

I knew that joint detention thing wasn't gonna work. I sighed. "Sure. Be right there." I left my groceries in the basket and headed to the school.

This time, I entered the counselor's office to find that the principal, Mr. Hanson, was present in addition to Ms. French. I was also shocked to see both Blair *and* Morgan sitting on the other side of the desk.

I frowned. "What's going on?" I asked.

"Ms. Dandridge, have a seat," Mr. Hanson said, almost as a demand.

I don't do well with demands or even "almost" demands. So I swung my Prada purse over my shoulder, crossed my arms over my chest, and said, "I'll stand."

"Fine. We have a problem here, Ms. Dandridge," Mr. Hanson said. He sounded like he was annoyed.

"Obviously, we do," I said, equally as annoyed.

"Your sons were involved in a fight today. *In detention.*"

I frowned. "Morgan didn't have detention."

He nodded. "Yes, ma'am. That's what's so ironic about the situation. Morgan went to the detention room and *started* the fight. Blair jumped in and helped him. They both teamed up against one boy."

I turned to Morgan. "Is that true?"

Morgan looked up at me and hesitantly nodded.

Oh, Lord. "Why, Morgan?" I asked.

"That Sam dude was talking trash outside the school this morning. Talking about how he was gonna kick Blair's butt in detention, and I wasn't having it," Morgan mumbled.

I sighed. "Morgan, didn't we talk about this? Didn't I say *no fighting*?"

He looked up at me with pleading eyes. "I wasn't gonna fight him at first, but he started talking trash to me. He said you should've stuck with your own kind. He said it would've been better if we were just regular niggers. He said a half-nigger terrorist was the same as a dog."

I blinked hard. What kind of child would say those things? I turned back to the pale faces of the principal and counselor.

"Ms. Dandridge, you see the dilemma we're in. We can't allow this type of rebellion to spread," Mr. Hanson said.

Whose rebellion? Sam's or my boys'?

I held my peace and nodded. "I understand. What's their punishment?"

"They will both be sent home for three days. No make-up work. One more incident and they'll be expelled," the principal said.

"Ok, and this Sam boy?"

"He'll have to serve the remainder of his detention."

I bucked my eyes. *"That's it?"*

Mr. Hanson raised his eyebrows. "Well, Ms. Dandridge, your sons have been the aggressors both times there was a fight. They're out of control."

My eyes widened. I could feel my face heating up. "What?! They're being tormented by a white supremacist in training. You mean to tell me there's no recourse for what that boy is doing to them?!"

"Ms. Dandridge, he isn't *doing* anything. They're just words. I know it must be hard for you as a single mother with two young sons, but they have to be taught to control themselves. They can't get into a fight every time someone says something that they don't like."

I shook my head. "Just words? This boy is bullying my sons. Look at their records. They've never been in trouble before. *Ever.* I doubt if Ms. Quimby can say the same for her son. And for your information, they're father is *very* active in their lives." *Single mother, my butt.* They were trying to turn my sons into some black ghetto statistic, and that was *not* happening.

Mr. Hanson's eyes flashed. I'd hit a nerve. "The other young man is being punished according to his actions. So are your sons."

"And what happens when they come back to school? What happens when this boy continues to assault them with his words? What do you expect them to do?"

"Report it."

"And what if he goes further? That's a very angry child."

"I think Sam is more talk than anything."

"What if he's not? I understand that he's been throwing objects at Blair and tripping him."

"Blair's never reported it. If we don't know what's going on, then our hands are tied to do anything about it."

"You want me to believe that a teacher doesn't notice a student throwing pencils in a classroom?"

Mr. Hanson's only reply was to shrug. It seemed that he didn't care all that much about half-niggers either. I stared at him for a moment, trying to formulate another argument. But I couldn't. I realized that I wouldn't get anywhere with him.

"Come on, boys, let's go." I stormed out of the office with Blair and Morgan trailing closely behind me. I climbed into my truck and dialed Wasif's number.

"Dr. W. Masood's phone," a voice said cheerily. *Probably a nurse.*

"Is Dr. Masood available?" My voice was shaky. I was mad

as hell.

"No, ma'am. He's in a procedure."

"Would you please ask him to call Ms. Dandridge? It's very important."

"Sure thing."

I hung up and slammed my fist against the steering wheel. "Damn!" I screamed.

I glanced in the rearview mirror and saw the worried looks on my sons' faces. "I'm sorry, boys. Let's just go home." They both nodded. I headed home, ordered Chinese take-out for dinner, and watched TV with the boys before finally going to bed. Wasif didn't call back, and I cried myself to sleep.

Chapter 5

"Whatever It Takes"

The three days passed pretty quickly, and to be honest, I kind of liked having the boys at home with me. Spending so much time alone got old with me and besides, spending time with my boys always made me happy. They were my pride and joy.

We went about our usual morning routine pretty smoothly the day they were to return to school. I hoped that the day would end as well as it had begun. I pulled up to the curb outside the school and smiled at them in the backseat. "Have a good day," I said, but I really meant, *try to stay out of trouble.*

Morgan hopped out first and then waited for Blair. Blair didn't budge but sat in the backseat with his head down. "You're gonna be late," I said.

He looked up at me with an expression on his face that literally broke my heart. His eyes shone with tears as he pleaded with me. "Please don't make me go back, Mama. *Please*. I don't wanna go back in there."

I blinked back my own tears. "You've gotta go to school, Blair. You need your education," I said softly.

He shook his head. "I can't go back, Mama. Sam sent me a message on Facebook. He said he was gonna get me. He keeps posting this racist crap on his wall about me. I don't wanna fight him anymore. I'm *tired* of fighting."

"Don't fight, baby. If he tries anything, just tell the principal," I said, knowing full well that that was a waste of time.

"Ma, they're not gonna do anything. I didn't tell you that they checked my backpack the other day like I'm actually gonna bring a bomb up in there. They're on his side!" His voice broke, and a single tear rolled down his face. He quickly swiped it away as if it were boiling hot.

I looked up at Morgan. He looked as if he was about to blow a gasket. If I sent them into that school, strike three was imminent. Expulsion was a guarantee.

As hard as I fought it, a tear rolled down my own cheek. "Get back in the car, Morgan," I said, my voice quivering.

Morgan dropped his backpack and balled up his fists. He shook his head. He was ready to fight. He almost looked like he could taste Sam's blood. He looked like he was ready to take on the entire school and its staff if he had to. I hopped out of my vehicle, ignoring the line of cars behind mine and the blaring of their horns. I walked around and picked up Morgan's backpack. "Morgan Masood Dandridge, *get in this car NOW!*"

He stood still, his eyes burning a hole into mine. If I let him walk into that school, Morgan may very well have killed Sam. I could see it in his eyes that were replicas of mine. The hate, the malice, the rage. Rage could give person superhuman strength. "NOW!" I shouted.

A tear fell from Morgan's eye as he whined, "*Maaaan!* Mama, let me get that dude!"

"NO! GET IN THE CAR!"

He climbed back into the truck, slammed the door shut, and slumped against the back of the seat. I breathed a sigh of relief.

I climbed into the driver's seat and let my own tears flow. "Oh, Lord!" I groaned as I covered my face with my hands.

"I'm sorry, Mama," Morgan said softly from the backseat.

I shook my head and wiped my face. "It's not your fault. Let's just go home so I can figure out what we need to do."

I tried to call Wasif three times after we got home, and I left three messages. He didn't call back, and to say that I was P.O.'d at him would be an understatement. Blair was upset, Morgan was homicidal, and I was a wreck. We needed Wasif, and he was nowhere to be found. My patience with him was really running thin.

♦♦♦

Wasif finally called back on Sunday. By then, the boys had been out of school for an entire week, and I was still trying to figure out what to do. One thing I was certain of, I was not sending them back to that school.

"Hello," I said. I only sounded half as irritated as I felt.

"Hey, babe. It's been a crazy week. Sorry I couldn't call earlier."

I rolled my eyes. "Yeah, me too," I said dryly.

He cleared his throat. "Um, what's going on? How are the boys?"

I rehashed the week's events to him. I could hear his belabored sigh after I'd finished. "I'm gonna home school them," I said. The thought had just occurred to me.

"You're not qualified for that, Mo. They need to be in school so they'll get into a good college. They'll just have to learn to deal with these things. They can't fight every time someone says something they don't like. And they can't run away from their problems."

"Wasif, you didn't see this boy, and you didn't see Blair. This kid is torturing him, and there's nothing the school can or will do about it. The boy's own mother can't control him. I can't send Blair back into that. And if I do, I'm afraid Morgan's gonna be the main one who gets in trouble. He's mad as hell."

Another sigh. "We'll discuss it tomorrow when I come over."

"There's nothing to discuss. I'm not sending them back there."

"You can't home school them, Mo."

"Then put them in a private school."

"What?! I can't afford that. I'm paying bills for two households as it is! Babe, do you realize that I spend more on you and the boys than I spend at home?" he said, raising his voice.

I stood up and began to pace the floor. "What in the hell is that supposed to mean?! Are we supposed to live like paupers just because you decided to go have another family?! You must have lost your whole entire damn mind! Did you forget that we were here first, Wasif?! Huh? Did you?!"

"Now wait a minute, Mo. That's not what I meant. I was just saying that private school would add to the strain. I'm stretched thin as it is, babe," he said, his voice calmer.

"But you can afford for your daughters to go to private school, right? I guess they're worth more to you than your sons are. Morgan and Blair don't mean crap to you, do they?"

"You know better than that. I'm just saying that money is getting tight, that's all."

"Well, I guess you need to find some more chests to crack open, Dr. Masood. Step up your business or something. You promised to take care of us. If you can't do it, I'll find someone who can."

"What is that supposed to mean?!" His voice had raised three octaves.

"Hell, you're smart, being that you're a doctor and all. Figure it out."

"Ok...ok, let's both calm down here before we say or do something we'll regret."

"I'm already calm."

A third sigh. "Can we just discuss this tomorrow, babe?"

"Fine. Bye, Wasif."

"Bye. Love you, Mo."

I hung up without returning the sentiment on purpose. I knew he'd be upset about it. He always needed to hear me say the words. He always wanted to be reassured that I still loved him despite our situation. He hadn't offered me any reassurance, so I was just returning the favor. I knew that when he came over on Monday, he'd give in. I even half-expected him to show up with a ring or some other piece of jewelry in addition to the flowers he brought me every week. One thing's for sure: I knew how to get my way with Wasif Masood.

I spent the rest of the evening online, giving his Visa a good workout. After purchasing two dresses, a pair of jeans, three blouses, and two pairs of shoes, I settled into bed with a smile on my face.

Chapter 6

"I Apologize"

I had help cleaning up on Monday since the boys were home. In between our vacuuming, sweeping, and mopping, Wasif called my cell phone nearly every hour. I ignored the calls. After all, he'd ignored mine. That afternoon, I finally shut my cell phone off and silenced the ringer on the house phone. When he tried calling the boys' phones, I told them to tell him I'd call him back, but of course I never did. I figured I'd let him sweat it out. This way he'd know I wasn't playing about the private school.

Wasif made it to the house at five on the dot, just like every other Monday. We were having spaghetti and salad for dinner, Blair's favorite. Wasif didn't really care for spaghetti, another reason I'd cooked it.

I heard him walk into the kitchen but didn't turn around to acknowledge his presence. Lizzie trotted into the kitchen to greet him, her paws clicking on the linoleum floor. I heard him pet her and whisper something to her. Satisfied, she trotted back to the den. Behind me, Wasif cleared his throat. I pretended not to hear him, as if fixing plates had totally blocked out my hearing. He stood there for a few moments and finally let out a soft, "Hey, babe."

I turned around and tried to look startled, but Wasif looked so good in his navy blue business suit that it was hard to stay in character. I don't think I was very convincing. "Oh, hello. I didn't hear you come in."

He looked at me with concern in his eyes. "Oh...ok."

I turned back to the plates, and he walked up behind me. He wrapped his arms around me, and I wriggled out of his grip. "Dinner's ready," I said and walked past him into the dining room, a plate in each hand. I could hear him sigh all the way from the kitchen.

He followed me into the dining room. I glanced up from the table to see that he was holding a bouquet of red roses and a small gift bag. I kept setting the table. He was gonna have to work for my forgiveness.

"Babe, are you gonna act like this all night, the *one* night I'm here?"

"You act like that's my fault. You *choose* to be here one night a week." The words fell out of my mouth before I could stop them. I hadn't intended to say anything like that. I guess I was more upset with him than I realized.

Pain flashed in Wasif's eyes. "You know this is not what I want for you, for *us*. I'm doing the best I can, babe." I nodded and then breezed past him as I walked back into the kitchen. He followed me. "Mo, I'm sorry."

I turned around, looked at him, and cocked my head to the side. "For what?"

"For not calling back sooner. For not being here. For everything."

"What about the private school?"

"I made a call this morning. I had to agree to make a sizable donation to the school *and* serve on the board to get them in on such short notice, but they're in. You have a meeting with the administrator of the Central Arkansas Christian School tomorrow. Tuition's already paid."

I closed my eyes and breathed a sigh of relief. "Thank you."

He reached for my arm. This time I didn't recoil. "Why'd you hang up on me? Why've you been ignoring my calls?"

"I was upset. My boys needed help, and you were acting like you didn't care."

"*Our* boys. You know I care. I love them. They're my only

sons. There's nothing I wouldn't do for them. I just thought that maybe you were exaggerating a bit."

I scoffed, "Yeah, because I'm always exaggerating when it comes to them, huh? Whatever, Wasif."

He looked into my eyes and ran his fingers through my soft, naturally curly hair. "That's not what I mean. It's just that sometimes you can be a little overprotective with them."

I raised my eyebrows. "Don't you think one of us needs to be?"

He closed his eyes. "You're not being fair. I love the boys. I love you, Mo. I'm sorry things aren't perfect, but I'm *trying*." There was desperation in his voice like I'd never heard before. I was suddenly sorry for acting so cold towards him.

I reached up and rubbed his cheek. "You're a good man, Wasif, and you've done more than good by me and the boys. I love you, too."

There was relief in his eyes. He'd finally heard the words he'd been waiting to hear. He kissed me and then hugged me tightly, as if he was afraid of letting go.

"Let me get the boys so that we can have dinner. I know you don't particularly like spaghetti. Sorry." I gave him a sheepish look.

He released me and shook his head. "Spaghetti's great.

These are for you." He handed me the bouquet and the bag.

I smiled. "Thank you." I peeked into the bag and unearthed a small blue box. Inside was a pair of diamond and onyx oval hoop earrings. "They're beautiful," I said. I kissed his lips softly. Just as I was about to pull away from him, he pulled me closer and continued the kiss.

When he finally released me, he said, "I love you so much, Mo. I don't wanna lose you."

I looked him in the eye. "You won't," I said, and I really meant it.

Wasif smiled at me and then headed in the den to get the boys for dinner. Over dinner, he talked to both Blair and Morgan about the events of the past couple of weeks. I couldn't help but to smile at their father-son interaction. I was so glad that my boys had Wasif for a father.

Evidently, Wasif had a point to prove. After dinner and TV with me and the boys, Wasif led me to the bedroom and showed a side of him that I'd never seen before. If he kept that up, I may never let him leave my bedroom again. I think that if he hadn't had surgery scheduled the next morning, we would have stayed in bed all day. I can't say that I would've minded at all.

The next morning, I walked into the twins' new school dressed in a Michael Kors black and white polka dotted wrap dress and a pair of ridiculous Kenneth Cole black pumps. I also wore the earrings Wasif bought me and the huge oval diamond ring he'd given me for my birthday the previous year. I was dressed to impress, thanks to Wasif's Visa card.

Mrs. Leon, the administrator, was nice enough. After I'd completed the enrollment paperwork for both boys, she took me on a tour of the school. It consisted of two buildings, which combined, held classes for grades K3 through twelve. Included on the campus were a small gymnasium and an even smaller playground. No football field or football team, odd for a southern school. Surrounding the school was an immaculate green lawn with rolling hills. Twenty acres, Ms. Leon informed me.

Average classroom size was ten to fifteen students, serving as "an incubator for optimal learning," a direct quote from the school's brochure. Average ACT score was a thirty-two. Ninety-eight percent of the previous year's graduates were accepted into Ivy League Colleges. Alumni included a senator, a federal judge, and several prominent lawyers and physicians. Proper training ground for Dr. Masood's children, even if he was only listed as an emergency contact on the enrollment forms. I'd left the paternal information blank, just as I always did. It wasn't any of their business.

I thanked Ms. Leon and left with a promise to have the boys there the next day, on time and in full uniform. I was happier than I'd been in weeks.

Chapter 7

"How Does it Feel?"

I sat outside the school and waited for my boys to be dismissed. They'd been attending the new school for two weeks, and they were adjusting well. I felt relieved that things had calmed down. I didn't miss those mid-day phone calls from the counselor or principal, and I definitely didn't miss young Sam Quimby or his racial slurs.

Blair was the first to emerge from the building with the pack of khaki-and-red-clad kids. Just seconds after the bell rang, he came bounding out to the car with a grin on his face. I loved seeing that smile. "Hey, Mama," he said as he climbed into the backseat.

I turned and smiled at him. "Hey, Blair," I said. "Good day?"

He nodded. "Yes ma'am."

Ten minutes passed before Morgan finally exited the school

and approached my window. I felt a sinking feeling in the pit of my stomach. *Oh Lord, what's going on?* I frowned as I rolled the window down. "Morgan, what's wrong?"

He smiled, revealing two even rows of white teeth, proof of regularly scheduled dental visits. "Nothing. The basketball coach wants to talk to you about me and Blair."

"The basketball coach? Now?" I really hadn't planned to get out of the car until I made it back home. I almost drove to the school in my house clothes. I sighed. *Good thing I decided to fully dress.* I was wearing jeans and a UCA sweatshirt. I guessed that I looked decent enough. I looked back at Blair wearing earbuds in his ears and bobbing his head to some music. I waved at him to get his attention and then gestured towards the school "Let's go." Blair nodded and then hopped out of the car.

I walked towards the entry flanked by my two sons. I smiled as I noticed Blair's lazy gait. He walked just like Wasif. Morgan walked with his shoulders squared, exhibiting the posture of someone full of confidence.

We walked through the school to the gym, which was connected to the small cafeteria. There were scriptures written in calligraphy on the white walls of the gym. The oak floor shone brightly, reflecting the lights overhead. I could see the coach leaning over, placing red, white, and blue basketballs on a rack. He was tall, maybe 6'2", and very muscular. He exhibited pure power. He must've logged in several hours a week at the gym. He wore black track pants and a tight black t-shirt. His arms were so huge, it looked like they were going to burst out of their sleeves. From that angle, I had a perfect view of his perfect butt. Now, I loved me some Wasif, but this man was *fine!*

We were only a few feet away from him when Morgan said, "Coach, this is our mom."

The coach turned around and faced me with a bright smile. *A handsome face to match that body. Mm mm mm.* He extended his hand. "Mrs. Dandridge?" he said, but as soon as the words left his mouth, his smile disappeared. His eyes changed. *Do I know this man?* "M…Mona? Mona-Lisa?" he said.

I was more than taken aback. I hadn't heard someone call me by my full first name in years. I searched his face for something familiar. It took me a minute, but I found it. His hair was cut close now. No glasses. No acne. His skin was now a smooth shade of copper. And he'd gained about fifty pounds of muscle. But I saw the same almond eyes. The same wide nose and full lips.

"Corey?" I asked.

"Ma, you know Coach?" Morgan asked.

I nodded slowly. "We went to college together," I said softly. Well, we did more than that.

Corey nodded in agreement and then looked at my boys, finally realizing who they were. Corey had been my boyfriend from the eleventh grade to my first year of college. He was still my boyfriend when I met Wasif, and he was still my boyfriend when I got pregnant with the twins. When I'd told him that the babies weren't his, he'd been crushed. Corey and I had only been together a few times, but from the time Wasif and I met, we'd spent more time in bed than out. I knew that the odds were more in favor of Wasif being the father than Corey.

I'd broken Corey's heart back then, and I knew it. He'd even talked about us getting married. He'd never proposed to me, per se. I think he just figured that we'd always be together. I'd thwarted those plans. My past was back to haunt me.

"Wow, you live in Conway, too? Small world," he said. He was avoiding my eyes. He was still hurt about what happened between us years ago.

"Uh, yeah. It is. You needed to talk to me?"

He nodded and pasted on the fakest smile I'd ever seen in

my life. Looking me in the eye, he said with an official tone, "Um, yes. I noticed your boys playing around on the court during lunch. They've got some skills. I'd like them on my junior high team. I wanted to get your permission."

I shrugged. "Sure, if that's what they want."

"You don't need to discuss it with your husband first?" He was fishing. I'm sure it wasn't lost on him that the boys and I all went by my maiden name. He wanted to know if Wasif and I were still together.

"Their father is fine with whatever I decide," I said.

He looked away from me. "Well, good. Practice is Tuesdays, Wednesdays, and Thursdays directly after school until five. Games are Monday evenings."

"Ok." I turned to the boys. "You guys go on to the car. I need to speak with the coach alone." I handed my car key to Blair, and the boys turned to leave.

Corey smiled again. This time it was genuine. "Ok, guys. See you tomorrow after school. Be ready to work hard."

Morgan and Blair both wore huge grins as they said, "Yessir!" in unison.

I waited until they were out of earshot and then said, "Um, how've you been?"

He shook his head. "You didn't send those boys away so

you could trade niceties with me. What's on your mind, Mona-Lisa?"

I almost cringed at hearing my full name again. "Well, I guess I never said I was sorry for what happened between us back in college. I hope you're not still mad at me for it."

He smiled and almost laughed. "You think I'm still mad about that? What, Mona? You think I'm gonna take it out on your kids?"

I shrugged. "I don't know. Stranger things have happened."

He raised his eyebrows. "*Really*, Mona? I guess you've erased everything about me from your mind. I've always loved kids. Remember?"

"A lot of years have passed, Corey. I didn't know if you had changed or what."

"I see you haven't, huh? Still with Kareem?"

"Uh, you mean Wasif?"

"Yeah, him. You two married now?"

I dropped my eyes, suddenly feeling ashamed about my relationship with Wasif. "We're together, but we're not married."

He raised his eyebrows. "What's it been? Fourteen or fifteen years? Now *that's* a long engagement."

I sighed. "Look, Corey, I'm not here to discuss my

relationship with Wasif. I just want to be sure that we're on the same page when it comes to my sons."

"Yeah, well, your boys seem like good kids. I'd never mistreat them."

I nodded and then stood there like an idiot, trying to figure out what to say next. "So, you're a coach. I thought you always just wanted to teach."

He nodded. "I teach history and coach basketball and baseball as well. It's a small school, so most of the teaching staff has to take on multiple roles."

"Oh, I see. You been teaching long?"

He shrugged. "I've been teaching for about six years. Before that, I was in the Air Force for a while."

"Oh wow. So you followed in your dad's footsteps, huh?"

"Yeah, for a little while I did."

I stood there for a few more seconds and then said, "Well, I guess I'd better be going. It was good to see you, Corey. You look good." *Real good.*

He smiled slightly. "Yeah, you too." I wasn't sure if he meant that it was good to see me, too or that I looked good, too. I also wasn't sure why I cared what he'd meant. I drove home with my mind preoccupied. What were the chances that Corey Sanders would be my sons' basketball coach? Actually,

I never thought I'd see Corey again, ever. *I bet he's got a nice wife and some beautiful kids.* I shook my head as I pulled into my driveway. *Why do you care about his life?* I walked into my house, and as hard as I tried, I couldn't get Corey Sanders out of my head.

◆◆◆

I wasn't having a good day. It was raining, I was coming down with a cold, and I could already see that the line at the drive-thru at Walgreen's was a mile long. Nevertheless, I pulled onto the parking lot, parked at the rear of the line, and waited. I was there to pick up my birth control, and then I was heading back home and back into my bed. I didn't feel like waiting, but birth control was a must. My pregnancy with the twins had been a hard one. I'd developed gestational diabetes *and* preeclampsia. I ended up spending the last two months of my pregnancy on bed rest, and I gained sixty pounds, twenty of which I was still holding on to, and I'd been thick to start with. So, I definitely had no plans of getting pregnant again. I'm sure Wasif was relieved about that.

After nearly an hour's wait, I pulled up to the drive-thru window and gave the clerk my name. She smiled and retreated into the pharmacy. When she returned, she was still smiling. "Ms. Dandridge, the pharmacist says that we're out of your medication. It'll be another week before we can refill it."

A week? I'd taken my last pill that morning. I would have to cut Wasif off for a while. I just didn't feel like driving to another pharmacy or anywhere else for that matter. "Ok, thanks." I headed back home. The boys had basketball practice so it was just me until five, and I had plans to sleep the day away.

Imagine my surprise when I made it home and saw Wasif's vehicle in my garage. It was a Wednesday morning. *What's he doing here?*

I walked inside the house and was greeted by an excited Lizzie. "Wasif?! Where are you?" I called as I petted her.

"Bedroom," I heard him say in a muffled voice.

I walked through the house to my bedroom. A smile spread across my face when I saw Wasif, lying naked in my bed. I felt better already. His gorgeous dark skin contrasted against my white comforter. What a beautiful sight. India Arie's "Brown Skin" played in my head as I stared at his body. He looked like a dream come true. *My* dream come true.

"It's not Monday," I said as I leaned against the door facing.

"I know. I wanted to see you. I *needed* to see you," he said.

I walked over to the bed, leaned over, and kissed him. "I'm so glad you're here. You're exactly what I need right now."

After Wasif showed me exactly how much *he* needed *me*, we lay in bed together in silence. He held me close to him. It felt good to be with him in that way.

"How long can you stay?" I asked.

"As long as I want to. I called in sick. My dad's covering for me."

I laughed. "Doctors can't call in sick, Wasif."

"Well, I did. I missed you so much. I think I was going through physical withdrawal or something. I had to have you STAT."

I smiled. "I missed you, too."

"The boys still doing ok at the new school?"

"Yeah, they really are. They're on the basketball team. First game's Monday."

"Really? I never knew they wanted to play."

"Me either. The coach saw them playing at lunch and wanted them on his team."

"Wow, I'll have to be sure to make the first game."

I hesitated then said, "You'll never guess who the coach is."

"Who?"

"Corey Sanders."

I felt Wasif's body go rigid. His grip on my waist tightened. "As in your *ex-boyfriend*, Corey Sanders?"

I nodded against his chest. "Small world, huh," I said, repeating Corey's words.

"Yeah, small world," Wasif said, barely above a whisper.

We lay there quietly for a few moments and then I said, "Why don't you ever speak Punjabi around me?"

He laughed. "Because I figured you'd like to understand what I'm saying to you, babe."

"Why don't you teach me?"

"Really?"

I looked up at his face. "Really."

"Ok, let's start with something simple." He rolled over on his stomach, kissed my hand, and said, "Hand. *Hath.*"

I smiled. "Hath."

He kissed my arm. "Arm. *Baan.*"

"Baan."

He kissed my armpit and I giggled. "Armpit. *Kassh.*"

Through my giggle I said, "Kassh."

"Mmm, shoulder," he said as he brushed his lips across the skin of my shoulder. "*Mooda.*"

I closed my eyes. "Mooda."

I felt his breath on my neck. "Neck. *Garrdan.*"

"Mmm," I said. I think I forgot I was supposed to be learning the words.

He was face to face with me as he smiled and said, "My favorite. Mouth. *Mooh.*"

As he kissed me, I said, "Mm, mooh is my favorite, too."

He kissed me again and then looked into my eyes. "*Ki tussi mainu pyaar karde ho?*"

"What does that mean?"

"Do you love me?"

"How do I say, 'Yes, I love you'?"

He caressed my cheek and kissed the tip of my nose. "*Haan main tuhaanu pyaar karda haan.*"

"Wow. Ok, uh, haan main tuhaanu pyaar karda haan."

"You are such a good student."

"Well, you're a good teacher. What else can you teach me?"

"Um, I think it's time for recess. Are you ready to play?"

I smiled. "Yes, sir."

Chapter 8

"You're My Everything"

I sat in the bleachers and watched the practice in progress, and I have to say that my boys were actually pretty good. The way they handled themselves on that court, you'd think that they'd been playing for years. I'd been sitting there for about thirty minutes when Corey noticed me. He walked over to me with a smile on his face.

He sat down beside me and said, "They're good, huh?" His tone was much friendlier than it had been the other day.

I returned his smile. "Yeah, they are."

We sat there and quietly watched the kids play, and then Corey said, "How've you been, Mona?" He spoke so softly I'd barely heard him. Corey was the only person I knew who refused to call me by my self-assigned nickname, Mo.

"I've been great, Corey. How've you been?" I really wanted to know. I was sorry for the way things had turned out between us, but what do you do when you're in love? I'd loved Wasif almost from the first time I laid eyes on him. There's just no fighting that.

"I'm good. Your sons are some great kids. You've raised them well."

"Thanks. How are your parents?" Corey was one of those rare people who grew up in a loving two-parent home, complete with Sunday family dinners after church. I'd envied his life, his travels with his family, and their closeness. I spent a lot of time at their house when we were in high school, trying to soak up some of their normalcy, and his parents had always been kind to me.

He gave me a lopsided grin. "They're good. My dad's retired. I think he's about to drive my mom crazy, being around the house so much, but they're good. They live in Texas now."

"That's nice, Corey." He knew not to ask about my mom. He knew how I felt about her.

He grinned widely and nudged me gently with his elbow. Just that little contact sent a spark through me. What was that about? "So, you still like Blair Underwood and Morgan Freeman, huh?"

I nodded. "You still like Anita Baker?"

He laughed. "Yeah, you want me to sing a little something for you? I could do a little 'Angel' for you."

I shook my head and waved my hands. "Noooo. Please don't. "

"Aw, that hurt."

"Sorry, but I remember you murdering her songs back in the day. Unless a miracle has occurred, you can't sing a lick, Coach Sanders."

He shook his head. "Sad, but true." We both laughed.

"Gosh, we had so much fun together back in the day. We'd play music on your parents' stereo or watch music videos for hours after school. I loved it."

"Yeah, me too." There was a moment of silence, and then Corey said, "You still a big reader?"

"Yep."

"Yeah, I remember you always had your head in a book. I thought you had to be the smartest girl I knew to be able to read like that."

I smiled. "Really?"

He shrugged. "Well, yeah. That and the fact that you were with me. Any girl that chose me for a boyfriend would have to be smart."

I rolled my eyes. "Yeah, right."

He laughed. "We had a ball together, huh, Mona?"

I nodded. "Yeah, we did. You were such a great friend to me, Corey. The best."

"You were more than a friend to me," he said barely above a whisper.

"I know," was all I managed to say. I returned my attention to my boys and tried to forget how I'd hurt Corey.

He cleared his throat. "Um, Mona, I wanted to ask you something."

Oh no. Here goes. I looked up at him. "What is it?"

"I was wondering if I could take the boys to church on Sunday. It's kind of a team thing," he said.

Well, I wasn't expecting that. I nodded and contemplated his request for a moment. I went to church some when I was little, but I hadn't been in many, many years. What harm could come from it? "I guess so. What church should I bring them to?"

"Um, if it's alright I'd like to pick them up. That's kind of a team thing, too. We all ride together."

I nodded. "Okay. Um, what time do they need to be ready? Do you need our address?"

"Have them ready at 9:30. That way we can make it in time for Sunday School. I can get the address out of their files."

"Ok. No problem."

Corey smiled and then returned to the court full of sweaty boys. As I watched my boys run up and down the court, I felt a faint smile creep up on my lips. The notion of them going to church set well with me.

Chapter 9

"Men in My Life"

At 9:32 on Sunday morning, my doorbell rang. Morgan and Blair peeled past me in a blur as they raced to the door. They liked Corey. That was easy to see. And they liked being around him. Corey had a good rapport with the young men on the team. He was more of a big brother to them than a coach.

"Wait! Let me see you," I said as I trotted to the front door behind them. They were both wearing the black slacks and white oxford shirts I'd bought at Kohl's that Saturday. Their black dress shoes looked like they'd been spit-shined. I smiled proudly and hugged them both. "Be good."

"Ma, we're going to *church*. What could we do bad in church?" Morgan asked.

I opened the front door without answering him. On the other side stood a sight that nearly knocked me off my feet.

Corey Sanders was standing there wearing a navy blue pinstriped suit that fit him perfectly. His white shirt peeked from under the jacket. A red tie completed the ensemble. The heavenly scent of his cologne filled my nostrils.

With a bright smile he said, "Good morning, Mona. Are the boys ready?"

I just stood there with my mouth hung open. Corey was as fine as fine could get!

Blair and Morgan squeezed beside me and slid out the door. "Yessir!" Blair said.

"Great. I'll bring them back safely after church. Bye, Mona," Corey said.

I nodded. I was still speechless. I watched as Corey backed the school's van out of the driveway. It was full of boys of all races. I tried to remember the name of the church he was taking them to. I was still standing in the open doorway, recuperating from Corey's fine-ness, when Wasif pulled into the driveway. *Wow, three visits in one week?*

Wasif pulled into the garage, and I walked into the house to meet him. I heard him when he came in through the side door. "Mo! It's me."

I walked into the kitchen. "Hey. What's going on?" I asked.

"Missed my family," he said as he walked over to me and

pulled me into a tight hug. "Where're the boys?"

"Church. With Corey."

He stepped back and frowned. "Church? I thought we were going to let them choose a religion later on." Wasif was a non-practicing Muslim, and I was a semi-Christian. Wasif didn't eat pork or drink alcohol, but that's about as far as his religious commitment went. I tried to do what's right most of the time, but that was about it for me. Consequently, neither of us had been very passionate about what religion the boys chose.

I shrugged. "Well, Corey asked, and the boys said they wanted to go. So, I guess they chose. You just missed them. He picked them up a few minutes ago."

"So much for my plans then," he said, sounding and looking disappointed.

"What plans?"

"I bought a basketball goal. I was gonna put it up out back and play with the boys today."

"Aw, babe. That is so sweet! They'll be back after awhile. Church won't last all day."

He pulled me back into his arms and smiled. "Mm, then that means we have time to kill." He leaned over and kissed my neck.

I smiled. "Um, I'd like nothing better, but I ran out of birth control the other day. You wouldn't happen to have protection, would you?"

He shook his head. "No, don't need it. The drugs are still in your system."

I frowned. "You sure?"

"Babe, I'm a *doctor*. Of course I'm sure. It won't wear off for weeks."

I smiled. "Well, in that case..."

Wasif spent the next couple of hours teaching me more Punjabi, but this time, he didn't bother to translate. We finally emerged from my bedroom just minutes before Corey brought the boys home. Wasif was in the backyard attempting to assemble the basketball goal when they made it home. I was in the kitchen when I heard the doorbell. I peeked through the window and saw Wasif wipe sweat from his brow, a look of determination on his face. I smiled as I walked to the front door.

"Who is it?" I called through the door, knowing that it was the boys.

"Ma! It's us!" I recognized Morgan's voice.

I laughed as I unlocked the door. Both boys stood on the other side of the door wearing wide grins. Behind them stood

Corey Sanders, and he was *still* fine.

"How was church?" I asked.

"Great," Blair said and kissed me on the cheek before breezing by me.

"Yeah," Morgan agreed, kissing my other cheek. Instead of walking past me, he hovered behind me in the foyer.

I smiled up at Corey. "Thanks, Corey. I hope they behaved themselves."

He nodded. "Like I said, they're good boys. No problem. Maybe you could come with us next time."

"Yeah, Ma," Morgan said.

I glanced at Morgan. "We'll see."

"Ma, can Coach stay for dinner?" Morgan asked.

"Uh..." I said, choosing my words carefully.

Corey saved me. He smiled at Morgan and said, "Can't stay, Morgan. Got plans. Maybe next time."

Before me or Morgan could reply, Blair came running back into the foyer. "Hey, Morg! Dad's here!"

Corey's eyes narrowed as they shifted from my face to something behind me. I followed his gaze. Wasif had walked into the foyer. His shirt collar was drenched with sweat, and he was wiping his hands on a towel. He leaned over and kissed my cheek. "Who we got here, babe?" he asked. Wasif knew full well who Corey was.

"Dad, this is Coach Sanders," Morgan said excitedly then turned to Corey. "Coach, you *gotta* stay for dinner since my dad's here." I hated the way Morgan was making it sound like Wasif's presence in our home was rare, even if it was true.

I opened my mouth to speak, but Wasif beat me to the punch. "I'm sure Coach Sanders has other plans, son, maybe with his own family," Wasif suggested.

A smile crept across Corey's face. Not a friendly smile, but more of a devious one. "You know, now that I think about it, I don't have plans after all. I'd be glad to join you all for dinner."

Silence from me and Wasif.

"Great! Come on, Coach. Let me show you the goal my dad just put up for us!" Blair said.

"Goal?! Sweet!" Morgan said as they both took off for the back yard.

Corey stepped closer to me and said, "Thanks, Mona." He gave Wasif a lopsided grin as he followed the boys through the house as if to say, *check mate.*

"Babe, I'm gonna take a shower. You wanna join me?" Wasif spoke loud enough for Corey and all of the neighbors to hear him. Corey kept walking without turning around, but

I'm sure he'd heard Wasif. *This is going to be an interesting dinner*, I thought.

♦♦♦

The aroma of eggplant casserole filled the kitchen and most of the house. The boys had changed out of their church clothes and were both wearing basketball shorts and t-shirts. Wasif had actually been serious about the shower, but I'd declined his invitation. He'd changed into a pair of jeans and a polo shirt. As he sat down beside me, he leaned over and planted a long, lingering kiss on my lips. I might have been turned on if I didn't know the kiss was more for Corey than for me.

"Dinner smells good, babe," Wasif said. He was supposedly talking to me, but his eyes were glued to Corey.

"Sure does, Mona," Corey said from his seat across the table from me and Wasif. The boys were seated on either side of him. He'd shed his sport coat, and I could see his muscles as they bulged through the sleeve of his shirt. Good Lord, the man was fine! I had to make myself stop looking at him. I looked over at Morgan who was smiling widely and looking at Corey. He really liked Corey, more so than Blair, but they both liked him. Funny, Corey and Morgan almost had the same smile. I'd never noticed that before.

"Um, thanks," I said. *I will really be glad when this meal is over.*

"Hey, Kashif. You eat this kind of food?" Corey asked, mispronouncing Wasif's name on purpose.

Wasif smiled stiffly. "It's *Wasif,* and I like anything my beautiful Mona-Lisa cooks for me." He lifted my hand and kissed it, never taking his eyes off of Corey.

Corey shifted his eyes away from us.

There was a short period of awkward silence, and then Corey bowed his head, silently praying over his food. We all dug in and were enjoying a quiet meal until Morgan spoke up. "Hey, Dad. Ma said she and Coach knew each other in college. Did you know Coach, too?" He turned to Corey and added, "My dad graduated from The U of A."

Corey raised his eyebrows and nodded slowly. "Yeah, I used to see you around the union sometimes," he said as he pointed his fork at Wasif.

"Yeah," was Wasif's only reply. He never looked up from his plate.

"Yeah, what was your name again? Shareef? You were on the soccer team," Corey said with a smirk. He was doing a good job of getting under Wasif's skin, and he knew it.

Wasif shook his head as he looked up at Corey and with a

wry laugh said, "My name's Wasif, *Corky*."

The tension between them was obvious. Morgan and Blair looked from their father to Corey with confused expressions on their faces, unaware of the events of the past that linked the three of us.

Corey smiled stiffly and through his teeth said, "*Corey*."

With raised eyebrows, Wasif said, "Oh yeah. *Corey*."

"Dad, our first game's tomorrow. You coming?" Blair said.

Wasif smiled at Blair. "Wouldn't miss it, son." He turned his attention back to Corey. "Corey, these two boys are my pride and joy. There's no greater honor for a man than to be the father of sons. Do you have any kids? You married?"

Corey shook his head and looked Wasif square in the eye. "Nope, no kids, no wife. Haven't found the right woman yet. I had a good woman once, but she left me for some loser back in college."

I choked on my lemonade, and Wasif patted my back. Once I regained my composure, I gave Corey an icy glare. He gave me an innocent smile in return.

"You married, Wasif?" asked Corey. *Uh oh.*

This time, it was Wasif who nearly choked. I thought quick and said, "You boys want dessert or a few more minutes outside before dark?"

Reminding them of their new toy had taken the spotlight off of Wasif. Both boys answered me by jumping up from the table and running out to the back yard.

Wasif slammed his hand on the table and glared at Corey. "I don't know what you're up to, Sanders, but you need to cut these games out."

Corey smiled. "Games? I don't play games, Dr. Masood. It was an innocent question."

"Stay away from my family. *Thaanu merry sambaj aaie?*"

Corey jumped up from the table. "What the hell did you just say?"

Before Wasif could reply, his cell phone rang. He checked the caller ID, mumbled something else in Punjabi, and then said, "I gotta get this." He gave Corey one more glare before leaving the table.

Corey shook his head and sat back down. "So he's just gonna cuss me out in some foreign language, huh?"

I rolled my eyes and shook my head. "Aren't ethnic jabs a little beneath you, Corey? The food, his name, *really*?"

Corey shrugged. "Just having a little fun. Is it my fault if he can't hang?"

"Whatever, Corey. And why would you ask him about being married in front of the boys?"

He raised his eyebrows. "They don't know whether or not their father is married? I mean, I saw a ring on his finger." He leaned over and looked at my hand. "You said you two aren't married, so who's he married to, Mona?"

"That's none of your business. If the boys weren't so happy to be on that team, I'd take them off ASAP."

Corey's face softened. "Look. Your hubby or lover or whatever he is, started it. I'm sorry. Won't happen again. I like the boys, and I wouldn't do anything to hurt them." He stood from the table and added, "Thanks for dinner, Mona. I'll let myself out. Tell Morgan and Blair that I'll see them tomorrow."

I nodded and watched him walk out of the kitchen.

A few minutes later, Wasif returned with a frustrated look on his face. "Where's your friend?" he asked.

"He left."

"Good. Mo, I don't know how I feel about him being around the boys. Maybe they shouldn't be on that team."

I shook my head. "They love that team. I can't make them quit. Besides, he apologized."

"Yeah well, he better watch himself. Um, that was the hospital. I gotta go." He leaned over and kissed me. "I'll see you at the game."

I smiled up at him. "Ok." I walked him to the door and said, "What was that you said to Corey in Punjabi?"

Wasif shrugged. "I just asked him if he understood me."

"Well, he thinks you were cussing at him."

"Good, let him think it. Bye, babe."

"Bye." I closed the door behind him and released an exasperated sigh.

Chapter 10

"Talk to Me"

The bleachers in the small gym were nearly full of spectators when Wasif arrived, wearing a leather jacket over his green scrubs. The scrubs hung loosely from his thin frame. Wasif hadn't gained an ounce in the fifteen years we'd been together. He'd barely aged either. The wire-rimmed glasses he wore were the only indication that he'd aged at all. He climbed the bleachers, taking them two at a time, making full use of his long legs.

As he took a seat beside me, I felt my heart flutter. Except for our annual family vacations, this was the first time we'd been in public together since he'd been married. In the past, I'd had to attend baseball games or pee-wee football games alone. I was happy that Wasif had made it. I hoped that the boys were able to see him there.

"Hey, babe," Wasif said, barely above a whisper. He kept

his eyes on the basketball court.

I glanced at him and said, "Hey." That was extent of our conversation. We both sat in silence and waited for the game to start.

About five minutes later, the teams ran out onto the court to warm up. I smiled and waved as I spotted Morgan and Blair, running onto the court wearing their red, white, and blue Eagles uniforms. I resisted the desire to point them out to Wasif, but the smile on his face told me that he'd already spotted them. I continued to watch them proudly. They looked like mini professionals out there, shooting baskets, practicing passes, and dribbling.

I looked around the gym at the other parents as they proudly watched their children. I was thinking about how thankful I was to have my boys when I spotted Corey. He was standing under the goal at the end nearest my seat, watching the boys with his arms folded across his chest. He was wearing a red, white, and blue wind suit that matched his players' uniforms. I found myself wondering exactly how

Corey had managed to get so fine. In college, he'd been okay-looking. He was tall and thin, no muscles. He had a bad acne problem and wore thick glasses. Back then, I'd been attracted to his confidence and his drive. He was determined to do big things in his life. I'd needed to be connected to someone with goals and dreams. Especially with my upbringing.

I shut my eyes tightly and tried to delete any thoughts of my childhood. I'd worked hard to block out those memories. I refocused my attention on my boys. The past was the past. There was no sense in going back there. After all, I was having a pretty good present, wasn't I?

The game began, and the boys did well, *very well*. My heart leaped as I watched them sink basket after basket. Steals, assists, my boys looked like twin Kobe Bryants out there. I could feel the energy of Wasif's excitement as he watched our sons play with natural talent that neither of us could explain. I cheered until I was hoarse, and when the game was over, I bounded down the bleachers, leaving Wasif behind in my dust.

I ran onto the court and hugged both of my sweaty sons. "You guys were terrific! Where'd y'all learn to play like that?!"

Morgan grinned and shrugged. "I don't know. We just got it like that."

I raised my eyebrows. "You just got it like that, huh?"

"Hey, Ma. Where'd Dad go?" Blair asked. I followed his

gaze up to the bleachers—no Wasif.

I pasted on a smile, trying to mask my own disappointment. But then again, I guess I should've been grateful that he'd showed up at all. "He's probably on his way to the house. He'll meet us there. I know he's proud of you guys, too."

Blair nodded, accepting my answer. The boys left for the locker room, and I sat on the bench and waited for them. Minutes later, the team emerged from the locker room, led by Corey. He walked over to me with a wide smile on his face.

"They were great, right?" he said.

I returned his smile. "They sure were. I am so proud of them."

"You should be."

Morgan and Blair finally made their way over to me. "Well, good evening, Corey."

"Bye Coach!" The boys said in unison.

Corey laughed, revealing his perfect white teeth. "Bye boys. See you tomorrow."

♦♦♦

The next day, I walked around my house feeling like I was

floating on air. It turned out that I was right about Wasif. He was at the house waiting for me and the boys when we made it home. He had excitedly congratulated the boys and spent almost an hour talking basketball with them. Once the boys went to bed, he'd spent the rest of the night showing me so much love and tenderness, I thought I'd explode. It felt good to be able to spend so much time with him. It almost felt like we were a normal family. I couldn't help but wonder if maybe the sudden change meant that Wasif was thinking of leaving his wife. I'd pushed that thought out of my head long ago and had accepted things as they were, but his behavior as of late made me feel hopeful again.

I was lounging in the den watching TV with Lizzie sitting at my feet when I heard the doorbell ring. Lizzie barked in response. It was a little after noon. I walked to the door with a grin on my face, thinking that it was Wasif surprising me. I opened the door without checking the peep hole. I was surprised to see Corey standing on the other side.

With wide eyes I said, "Corey, what are you doing here?"

He raised his eyebrows. "Wow, good afternoon to you, too, Mona."

I shifted my eyes. "I didn't mean it like that. It's just that it's the middle of the day. Shouldn't you be at the school or something?" *Anywhere but here*, I thought. I felt strange around Corey, and the feeling didn't set well with me.

"I'm on my lunch break. I wanted to talk to you about Blair and Morgan."

I panicked. "W...what's going on? What happened?"

Corey shook his head and placed his hand on my shoulder. "They're ok. I just wanted to ask you something. Can I come in?"

I hesitated because, like I said, Corey made me feel strange. I couldn't explain it, but I didn't like it.

"Come on, Mona. What do you think I'm gonna do? Bite?"

I sighed. "Come on in." I led him to the living room and offered him a seat on the sofa. I sat across from him in my favorite recliner.

Corey eyed his surroundings. My living room was decorated in shades of gold and cream. It had an Egyptian feel to it, complete with gold pyramid paintings on the walls and Sphinx and Anubis statues. Every room in my house had its own theme. Italian for the kitchen, Asian for the dining room, tropical for my bedroom and bathroom, African for the den. The boys' rooms were the only ones I hadn't designed. I'd done the work all by myself, with the help of Wasif's money. Decorating was my favorite pastime.

"You've got a real nice place here, Mona. I meant to tell you that the other day."

"Thank you."

"You work?"

"No. What did you want to ask me?"

Corey shook his head. "Dang, aren't you a gracious host?"

I gave him a look that said *get on with it*.

He clapped his hands together. "Okey dokey," he said. "I wanted to talk to you about the boys.

"Ok..."

"I see a lot of potential in them. I just think they need a little more one-on-one attention. Morgan's full of aggression, and he just needs to pull it back a bit. And he's got confidence for days. Kind of reminds me of myself at that age. Now, Blair's smart but a little too passive. He could use a little of Morgan's aggression and a lot of his confidence."

I nodded in agreement. "Yeah, Blair's the brains, and Morgan's the brawn. Two halves of a whole. That's how they've always been."

Corey smiled. "Yeah, they complement each other. I think if I could spend a little extra time with them, I can really help them develop this natural talent they have."

"Ok, what do you want to do?" I asked.

"Is it ok if they stay an extra thirty minutes after the practices? I'd like to spend that time with just the two of them."

I shrugged. "I don't see a problem with it, as long as they have enough time to do their homework."

Corey smiled. "Great! Um, can I ask you another favor?"

I frowned slightly. "What is it?"

"Um, I need a team mother, and all of the other players' moms work."

I shook my head. "No way, Corey. I don't like kids unless I gave birth to them."

He laughed. "Come on, Mona. I just need you to help me chaperone during away games and keep the score book. That's it. The job comes along with a free ride in the front seat of the van."

I sighed. "Corey, I don't know. I'll have to think about it."

He nodded and then stood up from the sofa. "Fair enough. I better get back. Thanks, Mona."

"Thank you, Corey, for taking such an interest in my boys."

"No problem. They're good kids. I think they have bright futures."

I walked Corey to the door and watched him climb into his red Toyota Tundra pickup. I closed the door and headed back to my recliner. My mind veered into thoughts of high school. I remembered meeting Corey in my eleventh grade history class. He was the new kid in town. He'd moved to Jacksonville with his family. His dad was an Air Force man. At first, Corey was quiet, but when we were thrown together for a group project, I quickly learned how sharp he was.

We'd become fast friends and soon after that boyfriend and girlfriend. He was kind and respectful to me, something that I couldn't say about any male I'd ever met or known before him. I felt safe with Corey, and in my heart I knew he'd never hurt me. We were inseparable for those two years of high school, and when Corey chose to attend college in Fayetteville, he begged me to follow him, and I did. Like I said, I felt safe with him, and there was no way I was staying behind in Jacksonville with my mom and memories of the past.

I sighed. Jacksonville, Arkansas, felt a million miles away instead of what was in reality—just forty miles. I'd had to move back home when I was pregnant with the twins, but as soon as they were born, Wasif had begged his father to help me. In no time, he'd moved me and the boys into an apartment in Fayetteville. I haven't been back to Jacksonville since, not even to visit my mother. I'd cut off all contact with my past and tried my best to erase it from my memory.

I shook my head. I hated thinking about the past. I hated remembering where I came from, but being around Corey so much seemed like a constant reminder. Maybe that's why I felt so uncomfortable around him. I'd worked overtime to leave the past in the past, and now Corey was messing things up for me.

I was startled by the ringing of my cell phone. It was Wasif.

"Hello?"

"Hey, babe. Miss you," he said softly into the phone.

I smiled. "Miss you, too."

"I'm in the middle of rounds. I just needed to hear your voice. I love you."

"I love you, too."

"Ok, bye. Talk to you later."

"Bye."

I smiled as we ended the call. Just as he'd done so many years ago, Wasif took away all thoughts of my past life.

Chapter 11

"Mystery"

I finally gave in and agreed to be team mother. It didn't help my case that Corey told the boys about the offer. When I was their age, I would've rather died than have my mother traveling on school trips and ball games with me, but Blair and Morgan basically begged me to do it. Now, how was I supposed to turn them down?

Their first away game came on a Thursday. I sat quietly in the uncomfortable passenger seat of the school's van and listened to the team members chatter away behind me. They were a small team, which allowed for them to become pretty close-knit. I was glad that they'd accepted Blair and Morgan into their little family.

Corey hadn't had much to say to me other than "thank you," and I was grateful. I wasn't in the mood for much conversation. I wondered if Wasif would show up for the game in Tillar. He'd said that he'd try.

Corey tuned the radio to a gospel station and turned the volume down low, never taking his eyes off of the road. I inspected him from the corner of my eye. He was fine, alright. I shifted in my seat, feeling weird about my attraction to him. I wasn't even this attracted to him when he was my boyfriend. Now, all of a sudden, I was seeing Corey in a new light. It was almost as if he'd still been going through puberty when I knew him before. Now he was fully grown, and time had done him well.

I turned my head and gazed out the window. I told myself that no matter how fine Corey was, he couldn't compare to Wasif. Wasif was movie-star handsome, exotic, and passionate. He was successful, and he loved me. He was the father of my two beautiful sons. Wasif and my sons were all I needed in the world.

♦♦♦

The Dandridge twins, as the announcer dubbed them, were the stars of the game. Between them, they accounted for thirty of the seventy points the team scored. They didn't win the game, but Blair and Morgan were standouts nonetheless. I never spotted Wasif in the gym, and I have to admit that I was disappointed, more so for the boys than myself. I hoped I'd cheered them on enough for both of us.

After the game, Corey stopped at a fast food restaurant and got all of us meals before heading back to Conway. The ride back was a quiet one, with a visibly tired Corey keeping his eyes on the road. I turned the volume of the radio up a bit and let the gospel music lull me to sleep. Minutes later, I was awakened by a sudden jolt. I sat up straight in my seat and looked over at Corey. "What's going on?"

"I think we got a flat," he said calmly as he slowly pulled the van to the side of the road.

I turned and looked at the team members, who'd evidently been asleep as well. They all wore bewildered looks. Corey pulled to a stop and then stepped out of the van. I followed him and saw that the tire on the rear of the driver's side was indeed flat.

Corey shook his head. "Aw man," he groaned.

"Do you know how to change it?" I asked.

Corey gave me a look that said, *negro please.* "I used to fly planes in the military, Mona. I think I can handle changing a tire."

I shrugged. "*Sor-ry*, not all men know how." *Wasif doesn't.*

He began to unzip his jacket. "Humph, all *real* men do." He pulled his jacket off, and I darn near started drooling. "Hold this for me," he said as he handed me the jacket.

I needed to get away from him because I was too tempted to reach over and grab one of his biceps. "I'll get the boys out of the van."

"Yeah, they can watch. Like I said, all real men know how to do this."

I sighed as I opened the back doors. "Everyone out. Coach is going to teach you how to change a flat tire."

The boys complied, murmuring the whole time as they piled out of the van. I stood by, holding his jacket and resisting the desire to smell it. *Lord, what is going on with me? I have a man, I have a man…*

I watched as he explained to the boys what he was doing and patiently answered questions. The team never took their eyes off of him. They hung on his every word as if he was revealing some ancient secrets to them. They had nothing but respect for him. It was nice to see that he was such a good role model for them. Corey was just good, period.

Once Corey was finished, we all climbed back into the van. It wasn't long before I'd fallen asleep again. By the time I woke up, we were back in Conway, and Corey was pulling up to the school. I sat up in the seat and looked over at him.

"Sorry. I didn't realize I was so sleepy," I said, feeling a little ashamed for having left him to fight sleep alone.

He offered me half of a smile. "It's alright. I managed."

I climbed out of the van and waited with him as the other parents picked up their kids. When there was no one left but me, Corey, and my sons, I climbed into my car and started the engine. I waved goodbye to Corey and pulled off the lot. I made it home in minutes and crawled into bed, exhausted.

I was fast asleep, wrapped up in the sheets, when I smelled that familiar odor. It was so strong that I had to hold my nose to keep from throwing up. The stench of concentrated urine filled the air. I sat up and shook my sister. "Cleo," I said. "Cleo, you peed again."

Cleo sat up, her big round eyes full of tears. "I'm sorry," she whined.

"Come on," I said. I took her hand and led her to the bathroom, tipping softly by Mama's bedroom door. I turned the water in the sink on to a slow trickle. "Take your panties off," I said.

Cleo sat on the toilet and kicked out of her underwear. I washed the panties in the sink and gave Cleo a washcloth to clean herself up. I took one of the bigger towels and covered the spot on the couch where she'd had her accident. "You can sleep on my end," I told her.

I laid the wet underwear over the arm of the couch and lay back down with my little sister lying in front of me. We'd only been asleep a few minutes when I heard the slap.

"You pissed up my couch again, didn't you?!" I heard Mama yell. She yanked Cleo from the sofa by the arm. Cleo whimpered.

"It's okay, Mama. I took care of it," I said.

"Mmhmm. You go back to sleep. I told her if she did this again I was gone tear her up, and I meant it." Mama dragged Cleo out of the room to her bedroom and slammed the door behind them. I could hear the belt as it hit Cleo's skin over and over again. I could hear Mama screaming cuss words at her. I could hear the man in Mama's bedroom laughing. I covered my ears and cried.

I was still clutching my ears when I bolted awake in my bed. The memory of the horror I felt as a ten-year-old child was just as real as if it had happened that very day. I cried myself back to sleep.

Chapter 12

"Giving You the Best That I Got"

The next day, I felt a constant uneasiness. The dream had awakened memories that played over and over in my mind. For the first time in years, I wondered about my little sister. Cleo had run away when she was only twelve. I was sixteen at the time. I'd tried my best to shield her from our mother's abuse. I'd tried to take care of her, but she'd left anyway.

I probably would have left too, but by then, I'd met Corey, and his friendship had given me a reason to stick around. I wondered where Cleo was or if she was even still alive. I felt a tear trickle down my cheek. I hated revisiting that pain. I hated my past.

As I pulled my jacket on and slipped into my shoes, I wiped my face. It was time to pick the boys up from practice. I climbed in the car and drove to the school, my mind muddled. I had made it all the way to the gym when I realized I was actually too early. The boys had just begun their extra practice session with Corey. I sat in the car for a few minutes and then decided to walk into the gym.

I was still pretty much zoned out, but I kept my eyes on the court, at least giving the illusion that I was watching the boys. I didn't even notice when Corey walked over to me, but I felt him sit down beside me. Still, I kept my eyes on the court.

"You alright, Mona? You look like you've seen a ghost," he said. His tone was light, but he'd hit a nerve.

I frowned as I looked at him. I blinked back tears, but the catch in my voice gave me away. "I'm alright."

He stared at me for a few seconds, then I heard him tell the boys to keep practicing and that he and I would be right back. I wondered where we were going, but I didn't ask. I was relieved when he took me into his office and closed the door behind us. Before he could say a word, I collapsed against him and cried. He held me. No questions. He rubbed my back and whispered that everything would be alright. His words comforted me, even though I knew he had no clue as to what "everything" was.

I cried for a few minutes, standing there in Corey's arms, until finally, my tears ceased. I sat in one of the chairs in his office and accepted the tissue he handed to me.

"You wanna talk about it?" he asked softly.

"I dreamed about Cleo last night," I said as I wiped my face.

He squatted in front of me. "You still miss her?"

I closed my eyes. "Honestly, this is the first time I've thought about her in years. I've worked really hard at forgetting."

"She was a part of you. Maybe it's good to think about her sometimes."

I nodded.

"Can I pray with you, Mona?"

I looked at him, surprised. "Well...yeah, I guess."

He took my hand, bowed his head, and closed his eyes. I followed suit. I listened as he began to pray. "Dear Lord, please touch Mona. Heal her mind and her spirit. Mend her broken family ties and make her whole again. In Jesus' name, Amen." He opened his eyes and squeezed my hand in his. "Mona, if you ever need to talk, you know my number."

I nodded. "Thank you, Corey." We sat quietly in his office for a few moments so that I could pull myself together. I looked around the tiny room at the team pictures that hung on the wall and the trophies that lined the small bookcase behind his desk. The trash can next to his desk was full of fast food sacks and cups. It wasn't as nice as Wasif's office, by far, but it had a more inviting feel to it. The placard on his desk read, *Coach Corey Sanders*. I smiled.

"You ready?" He asked. I nodded. He held my hand as he walked me back out to the gym. When we walked back onto the court, I saw Wasif sitting in the bleachers staring at us. I froze in place and dropped Corey's hand. Corey looked at me, confused at first, and then he noticed Wasif. He sighed and shook his head. He walked over to the boys and huddled with them for a few moments. I walked over to the bleachers and sat down next to Wasif.

"What are you doing here?" I asked.

He turned and looked at me. He was visibly upset as he spoke. "You see those two boys out there, Mo? They're my sons. *They're* why I'm here."

I turned and faced him. "I didn't mean anything by the question, Wasif."

He frowned, finally noticing my puffy eyes. "You been crying, Mo?"

"Allergies." Wasif only knew the bare minimum about my life. He didn't deal with problems well.

"Oh, ok. You should get something for that." He accepted my excuse without any further discussion.

We sat quietly and watched the rest of the boys' practice. When they were finished, he followed me down the bleachers to them. They were both excited to see their father and nearly begged him to drive them home.

He smiled at them as he tousled Morgan's hair with his hand. Morgan was just a couple inches shorter than Wasif.

"You guys go on with your mom. I'll meet you at the house. I need to talk to Coach."

Oh no. I shook my head. "Why don't we all leave together? Me and the boys will wait for you."

He turned to me and kissed me on the cheek. "Why don't you go and get dinner ready, babe? I'll meet you there."

I hesitated for a moment, but then the boys' curious stares prompted me to leave. I knew Wasif wouldn't go too far with Corey. Corey outsized him by far. Wasif would be a fool to get into a physical confrontation with him.

Back at the house, I heard Wasif when he came in the door. He threw his keys onto the kitchen counter and released an exasperated sigh. I was bent over, peering into the oven at my chicken casserole. I turned to see that he was red-faced, wearing a look of frustration as he ran his hand through his hair.

"You ok?" I asked.

"We need to talk," he said, ignoring my question. He took a seat at the kitchen table.

I nodded. "Ok." I sat across from him.

"Is there something going on between you and Corey Sanders?"

I frowned as I leaned back in the chair. "Is that what he told you?"

"No. He said you two were friends and that you were helping him with the team."

"That's true. What did you say to him?"

"I told him how much you mean to me. How much I love the boys. I told him that we were a family and that nothing could change that."

I raised my eyebrows. "That's all you said?"

"Yeah." He was lying. I was sure he'd said much more than that.

I nodded and then stood and began gathering plates and silverware for dinner. Wasif walked over and hugged me from behind. "I love you, Mo. You'll never know how much. You'll never know how hard it is for me to leave you. How it hurts to have to keep what we have behind closed doors. Things will change. I promise you that."

I leaned against him and smiled. That was the first time

he'd ever said anything about our situation changing. "I love you, too, Wasif."

Though it was a Thursday night, Wasif didn't leave until the next morning. He ignored the ringing of his cell phone, eventually turning it off. I assumed it wasn't the hospital calling. He held me close all night long.

The next morning, he looked near tears when he had to leave. "I love you. I don't know what I'd do if I lost you," he'd said.

"You won't lose me," I'd answered. As I watched him leave, I really believed that things were about to change for us.

Chapter 13

"Plenty of Room"

Corey picked the boys up for church like clockwork on Sunday morning. He extended me another invitation to go with them, but I declined. I half-expected Wasif to show up, and when he didn't, I ended up falling asleep in my recliner while reading a book.

I had another dream. Actually it was more of a memory. One I'd long ago repressed.

This time I was younger. Maybe six or seven. Like I said, I'd worked hard to forget...

I'd just made it home from the bus stop. I opened the door. It was unlocked, as always. The sight of my mother naked on that sofa was just as clear as if it had happened only a few days earlier. On top of her was a man I'd never seen before. He was naked too, moving on top of her, making strange noises. I'd heard noises like that before from behind my mother's closed bedroom door. Now I had a picture to go along with the sound.

My Mama's eyes were closed. She was making noises, too. The man looked at me, but he didn't stop what he was doing. Cleo was sitting on the floor watching TV, her back to them. I grabbed her hand and led her to the bathroom. She resisted and whined about the TV. I was young, but I knew it couldn't have been appropriate for a two-year-old to be in that room at that moment.

We sat on the side of the tub, two sets of legs dangling, for what seemed like hours before the bathroom door swung open. The naked man walked in, glistening with sweat. While he stood in front of the toilet and relieved himself, his leg brushed mine in the cramped space of the bathroom. I shrunk away from him. He didn't bother to flush the toilet, and as he turned to leave the room, he stopped and looked at me, fully exposing his naked body to me. I looked up at his face with frightened eyes.

He gave me a lopsided smile and said, "Hey."

I said, "Hey" so softly that it was almost a whisper.

He left the bathroom, and a few minutes later, so did Cleo and I. Mama was sitting on the sofa, still naked. She was smoking a cigarette and watching the cartoons Cleo had been watching on TV. Cleo reclaimed her seat in front of the TV and smiled, satisfied to be watching TV again. I stood behind the sofa and looked at Mama. Finally, she turned and looked at me.

"Next time, knock. You don't ever know when I'mma have

company up in here."

I nodded.

"Oh, and that was your daddy. You shoulda said hey or something."

"I did."

"Good."

That night, when Cleo and I went to bed on that sofa, I could still smell my parents in the fabric. That was the one and only time I ever saw my father. I cried myself to sleep that night.

I was crying when I woke up on my recliner. That was just one more memory I'd worked hard to erase. Here it was again.

◆◆◆

When Corey arrived with the boys, I was still on the recliner. My eyes were swollen from having spent hours crying. I didn't even hear the doorbell ring, but thankfully I'd left the door unlocked. They let themselves in. I looked up to find Blair and Morgan, as well as Corey, standing over me.

"Mama, you ok?" Blair asked with eyes full of concern.

I nodded. "I'm fine," I lied.

"You sure?" Morgan asked.

Corey interrupted my next lie. "Why don't you boys go get changed? I wanna talk to your mom for a minute," he said. They both hesitated then left for their rooms. Corey pulled an ottoman to the foot of the recliner and sat in front of me. He took my hand in his.

"You been thinking about Cleo again?" he said softly.

I nodded. "And my mama. I had another dream."

"About what?"

"About the time I met my father." I'd told Corey the story when we were in high school. He knew just about everything about my past. He'd been my only true friend back in the day. He was the only person I'd ever confided in.

He looked at me with eyes full of compassion. "I'm sorry you had to revisit that."

My eyes filled with tears again as I nodded. "I've worked so hard to forget."

He nodded. "I can see that you've done a lot to erase your past. Maybe that's the problem."

"What do you mean?"

"Maybe you need to confront your past instead of trying to shut it out. Maybe if you keep trying to forget, it'll just keep popping back up."

I shook my head. "How can I live with these memories,

Corey? I don't wanna hate my mother, but I can feel it coming back. The hate."

Corey rubbed his thumb across the top of my hand. "Mona-Lisa, come to church with me tonight."

"What's that gonna fix, Corey?" I scoffed.

He shook his head. "I'm not saying it will 'fix' anything, Mona. But I do know that there's healing in the Word, and you definitely need some healing."

I dropped my eyes. "I don't know…"

Corey lifted my chin with his hand and looked me in the eye. "Please, Mona-Lisa. Just come with me this one time."

I nodded and sighed mournfully. "Ok. I'll go this one time."

He smiled then stood, leaned over, and kissed me on the cheek. "Good. I'll pick you up at 5:30. You don't have to dress up."

I bit my lip and looked up at him. "Um, maybe I should just meet you there. Wasif's really been acting paranoid lately."

Corey stood up straight and towered over me. "I'm not worried about Wasif. I'll pick you up."

"What did he say to you the other day?"

Corey laughed. "Something about getting me fired if I didn't stay away from you. He boasted about being on the school's board."

My eyes widened. "What?! He threatened you?!"

Corey took my hand in his and shook his head. "I'm not afraid of his threats. Nothing's gonna keep me from helping you. See you at 5:30, Mona."

I nodded. "Ok," I said and watched him out of the room.

Corey's church turned out to be the same church that owned and operated the private school. It was a huge multicultural mega-church. As I settled into my seat, sandwiched in between Corey and the boys, I took in my surroundings. I realize that we were well into the new millennium, but I was still amazed to see blacks, whites, Latinos, and Asians all sharing pew chairs. I imagined that the sanctuary was a snapshot of what Heaven would look like.

Corey grasped my hand and smiled at me. "You ok?"

I nodded. "Yeah."

I hadn't been to church since I was a girl. Back then, my grandmother, my mother's mother, would take me. She was my only link to the church and to God. When she moved out of state, I'd lost that connection. Church and God were the last things on my mother's mind. I looked at my sons sitting next to me. They were talking quietly to one another. I smiled and squeezed Corey's hand. Just sitting in that church made me feel a little better.

Music began to play, and the choir began to sing. I stood with the rest of the congregation as they began to worship God and closed my eyes. The music was beautiful, and the mood was so peaceful. I listened as they sang about God's greatness and wished that I understood more fully what they were talking about.

The choir sang worship music for a solid twenty minutes. The music was beautiful, and the atmosphere was heavy. I opened my eyes and looked up at Corey a few times. He kept his eyes closed and his arms raised, as if he'd shut out everything but God. I wondered what he was feeling.

The pastor finally stepped onto the platform and asked everyone to be seated. He was a tall, thin, handsome man. At first glance, it was hard to pinpoint his ethnicity. He could've been biracial or Hispanic. He appeared confident, and his voice was soothing. I listened attentively as he brought that evening's message.

"Good evening, brothers and sisters," he began. "This evening's sermon will come from a passage of scripture found in First Peter, chapter five and verse seven. 'Cast all your anxiety on him because he cares for you.' I have entitled this message: 'Give it all to Him.'"

I straightened up in my seat and glanced at Corey with a

smile on my face. He gave me a knowing look. It was as if the pastor knew I'd be there. As if he knew what I needed to hear. I kept my eyes on him throughout the entire message. I tried to commit every word to my memory. He said that God loves us, *all of us*, no matter what we've done or who we are. He said that God desires to carry our burdens for us. That He wants us to trust Him with them. He said that we should never feel alone with our troubles, that God is always with us and will never leave us.

That was when I understood what people meant when they said that God was an "on-time God". That sermon was what I'd needed to hear at that particular moment. After the sermon, I went to the altar for prayer. Corey went with me, never letting go of my hand. I went to bed that night with a sense of thankfulness in my heart. I slept better than I had in weeks. No dreams invaded my rest.

Chapter 14

"Body and Soul"

The next couple of weeks were busy ones for the team. I travelled to several out of town games with them and really enjoyed the time with the boys and with Corey. Being around a man who was that confident, calm, and caring was nice. Don't get me wrong, Wasif was a good man and a good father, but there was just something different about Corey, something special. He had a way about him that made me wonder why he wasn't married with kids. He was definitely a good catch. Watching him in action with the team was amazing. I have to admit, I was enjoying my job as team mother.

Tournament season hit, and the team was invited to several of them, including one in Pine Bluff, seventy miles from Conway. We travelled to Pine Bluff in the trusty van. The boys won their first game on that Friday night, and after spending the night in a hotel, the team was scheduled to play again that Saturday morning.

I'd settled into bed in my room that Friday night when I heard a knock at the door. I got up and checked the peep hole. It was Corey. I opened the door. "Hey, what's up?"

He smiled as he walked into the room wearing red pajama pants and a black t-shirt. I turned and walked over to the bed and took a seat. "You wanna sit down?"

He leaned against the closed door and crossed his massive arms across his chest. "No, that's ok. I was just doing room checks, and I didn't want to leave you out. Everything ok in here?"

I nodded. "Sure. I'm fine. Thanks for checking."

"You been having any more dreams?"

I shook my head. "No, not since the last one, thank goodness."

"Good. Well, I'll let you get some rest."

I walked to the door to let him out. We both reached for the doorknob, and our hands touched. I felt a spark that spread from my hand throughout my entire body. Corey felt it, too. We stood there and stared at each other for what felt like an eternity. The attraction between us was undeniable. I cleared my throat and was about to speak when Corey pulled me into his arms.

I managed to utter a simple "uh" before I felt his lips on mine. In an instant, the world around me disappeared, and there was only Corey. I wrapped my arms around him and returned the kiss. The only thought in my mind was, *WOW*. I can't lie; I wanted me some Corey Sanders right about then. For some reason, I felt at home in his arms, and it felt so good to be there. *Corey* felt good, better than I'd remembered. He finally released me and, breathing heavily said, "Mona..."

My eyes were glued to his. "Yes?" I whispered. *Whatever you want me to do, I'll do it. I swear I will.*

"Mona—"

My phone rang, interrupting him. I knew instinctively that it was Wasif, but I didn't care.

He gently caressed my cheek with the back of his hand. "You'd better get your phone, and I'd better leave."

"No, don't go," I said before I realized it. The phone began to ring again.

Corey searched my eyes. "Why?"

"B...because I want you to stay."

The phone continued to ring. "Wait," I said, then walked over to the night table and turned my phone off.

Corey nodded towards the phone. "Was that your baby

daddy?"

I laid the phone down and walked back over to Corey. "It doesn't matter who it was. Will you stay?"

His eyes never left mine as I approached him and laid my hand on his huge arm. "And do what?" he asked.

Whatever you want to do, however you want to do it. "Just be with me. *Please.*" I kissed him on his cheek.

He sighed as I took his hand in mine. He followed me to the bed, and we lay down together. Corey never laid a finger on me that night. We never even took our clothes off, but I can honestly say that I've never felt so close to a man before in my entire life.

Wasif was very upset about not being able to reach me that night, and I spent half of the next day convincing him that everything was fine between us. I was lying to him, and he knew it. Corey Sanders was inching his way into my heart, and I was sure that Wasif knew that, too.

◆◆◆

As the days passed, I found myself spending more and more time with Corey. I was at every practice, every game, church on Sundays, and I'd even begun to attend Wednesday night services with him. The more I was around him, the more I liked him and the more I could tell that he liked me. It was in his eyes. His eyes told me things that he never said with his mouth. I loved his eyes. I loved — wait, what was going on with me? What was going on between me and Corey?

One particular Sunday, Corey and I walked out of the church with smiles on our faces. Another awesome worship experience and another touching sermon had rejuvenated both of us. As the entire team of boys trotted to the van ahead of us, he took my hand in his. I smiled up at him.

"Lunch?" he asked.

I nodded. "I'd love to."

I stared out the window as he pulled off the church parking lot and smiled. Yeah, I liked being with him a lot. I realized that I'd missed him all those years we were apart. I was happy around him. *He makes me happy. That's what it is. I'm happy when I'm with him.*

As he pulled the van onto the lot at IHOP, I looked at him and raised my eyebrows. "Breakfast?"

He smiled. "Whatever you want." He stared into my eyes, and I felt my cheeks begin to heat up. I wanted to look away but couldn't. Honestly, I guess I really didn't want to look away, but I knew I should've wanted to. The sound of the boys opening the side door to the van shook us both back to reality.

I stepped out of the van and followed Corey and the team into the restaurant. We sat in a private section and dined together. The boys excitedly chatted with Corey and with one another. Corey was a natural with them, and they seemed to be totally at ease around him.

After lunch, I rode with him to drop off the team members and when we reached my house, I invited him in. He played basketball with the boys for a while, and then came inside for a drink of water. I sat at the kitchen table across from him and watched him drink. Actually I was staring at him like a lunatic stalker. *What is wrong with you?* I asked myself silently.

"It's not nice to stare," he said and then looked me in the eye.

Startled, I dropped my gaze. "I wasn't staring," I lied.

He smiled. "Yes you were, Mona-Lisa. I felt your eyes on me. You like to look at me, don't you? Quite a difference from how I used to look, huh?"

I couldn't answer. I was both embarrassed and intrigued. I crossed my legs and clasped my hands in my lap.

Corey watched my every move. "You, on the other hand, look the same." He paused, and I saw his eyes take me in inch by inch, head to toe. I placed my hand on my chest and tried to calm my throbbing heart. "Mmhmm, same hips and thighs, same lips and eyes. Damn, girl. You're *still* fine."

You, too. I shook my head. "I've gained weight," I said softly.

He smiled. "In all the right places."

Corey may as well have undressed me right then and there, because the heat between us was palpable. I adjusted in my seat and looked away from him again. He reached over and pulled my face back towards his. "You wanna look? Then look. I don't mind, but you have to let me look, too."

I stared at him for a moment. We stared at each other, actually. Finally, it got to be too much for me. *He* was too much for me. I stood and walked over to the counter. I had to put some space between us. I leaned against the counter and ran my hand through my hair. "Corey, do you have a girlfriend?" I don't even know where that question came from. I shouldn't have asked it. After all, I had a man—a good man. Why did I care?

"No," he said. His eyes never left me. "Why?"

I shifted my eyes. "I...I was just wondering."

He stood and walked over to me. He stood so close to me that I could feel his breath on my face. I glanced out the window at the boys in the backyard. They were still playing ball, oblivious as to what was going on between me and Corey. Corey smelled so good. *What's the name of his cologne? I'd like to buy some and spray it all over my sheets. Mmm.*

He traced my eyebrow with his fingertip. "Were you looking to apply for the position, Mona-Lisa?" he asked. He ran his finger over the bridge of my nose.

I tried to avoid his eyes, but they were like magnets to mine. "Um...uh...w....why haven't you ever been married?" I answered his question with another of my own.

He smiled as his finger softly blazed a trail over my lips to my chin. He shrugged. "Good question. Why haven't *you* ever been married?"

Good question. "I..." My voice trailed off as I tried to find an answer.

He smiled and lifted all 170 pounds of me up off the floor, sitting me on the tiled kitchen counter. He leaned in and softly kissed my neck. "Mm, you smell good, Mona. You smell so, so good," he murmured huskily. He rubbed his hands up and down my back and said, "You feel good, too." *I love Wasif, I love Wasif, I love...*

I gripped the edges of the countertop and searched his eyes as he pulled me into a kiss so passionate that I think I nearly lost consciousness. I couldn't think or breathe. He held me tightly and I melted in his arms. I guess I forgot that my sons were in the backyard or that Wasif had a key and could come into the house at his whim. I guess I'd forgotten about Wasif altogether. *Wasif, who?* All I knew at that moment was Corey and how he made me feel. I hugged him tightly and returned the kiss. Our passion was flammable—no, combustible. I'm honestly surprised that my kitchen didn't go up in flames at that very moment. Corey Sanders definitely knew how to kiss well, better than I remembered.

The sound of one of my sons yelling at the other in the back yard jarred us out of our bliss. Corey ended the kiss, stepped back, and smiled at me. "Did you like that, Mona?"

I nodded in response, because I honestly couldn't speak.

"Would you like another one?"

Again, I nodded, never taking my eyes off of his face.

He leaned in and this time gently brushed my lips with his, almost teasing me. I reached for him, eager to continue the kiss.

He backed away from me and smiled again. "You see what you've been missing, girl?" he asked softly. He slowly rubbed his finger across my bottom lip. "You see what you could have?"

I stared at him in silence. *Yeah, and I want it, too.*

He read my mind. "I'm not like Wasif. I won't be with another man's woman, Mona-Lisa. No matter how bad I want her. When you want something real, let me know." He kissed me softly again and then left the kitchen and returned to the back yard. I sat on the counter and fanned myself. *Lord have mercy!*

Chapter 15

"Been So Long"

It was a Monday afternoon, Wasif's day, and he called to inform me that he would be picking the boys up from school. He also told me not to worry about dinner, and I didn't. I needed a break. There were so many things swirling around in my mind. Corey, the dreams, my past, my present. So, I was thankful for his thoughtfulness.

That evening, Wasif and the boys made it home with pizzas and DVDs in hand, a couple of action flicks for him and the boys, and *Seven* and *Just Cause* for me. We had a nice family night and later on, Wasif and I had a nice time alone. I fell asleep to Wasif whispering promises of a future as husband and wife into my ear. You'd think I'd have had sweet dreams that night. But I didn't.

The dream I had that night came in the form of another memory that I had long buried.

I was fifteen. We had just moved into a duplex and instead of sleeping on the sofa, Cleo and I now had a bedroom to share. We got Mama's old bed, and no matter how many miles she'd put on it, it was better than sleeping on that sofa. Mama had bought herself a new bed. We'd been in that duplex about a week when Mama decided to throw a party. She invited several of her friends, male and female, all hard drinkers. Marijuana smoke clouded the air as the party went into full swing.

Cleo and I closed ourselves up in our room. All of a sudden, I could remember that night so clearly. It was raining. I was sitting on the side of the bed reading a book as the rain slid down the window pane. Cleo was watching the little 13-inch TV Mama had bought for our room. Around midnight, we'd both crawled into bed and fallen asleep, but the party was still rolling on.

I remember the door opening late that night. I remember Mama telling us to get up. Her friend Quan needed to sleep off his buzz. She gave him our bed and told me and Cleo to sleep on the floor. Cleo fell right back to sleep after we'd made the pallet on the floor. I lay awake for a long time, listening to Quan snore. Something about that grown man sleeping in the room with us just felt wrong to me. I'd decided to stay up and watch him. Nevertheless, I ended up drifting off to sleep, despite my efforts to stay awake.

It was the early morning hours when a sound woke me up. It sounded like crying, no, more like whimpering. I opened my eyes and *rolled over to find Quan on top of my eleven-year-old sister. She was crying, trying to push him off of her. I sprang up and grabbed one of my school books. A big, thick History book. I hit Quan over the head probably about ten times before he finally rolled off of Cleo and punched me in the nose. We fought, or should I say he beat me, for a few minutes before Mama finally came into the room and broke it up. Cleo and I screamed our explanation of what had happened, and I was relieved when Mama told Quan to leave.*

Mama walked him to the door. She came back into the room and looked at us. "I hope yo' nose ain't broke," she said. "And Cleo, you need to stop being so fast. He told me that you was rubbing up on him and stuff. You ain't got no business acting like that with a grown man." Before either of us could object to what she'd said, she left the room, slamming the door behind her.

I woke up with a start. It was when I saw Wasif lying next to me that I realized it was a dream. I sat there and watched the even rise and fall of his chest. He slept like he didn't have a care in the world. I grabbed my cell phone from the nightstand and tip-toed into the bathroom. It was one in the morning when I dialed Corey's number.

"Hello? Mona-Lisa?" he said groggily.

"Corey, I'm sorry to wake you. But I had another dream," I said softly.

"You want me to come over?" he asked without hesitation.

I shook my head. "No...no, can I come to you?"

"Mona, it's the middle of the night. You shouldn't be out alone."

"I'll be ok. Please...just let me come over there. Let me come to you."

He paused, probably realizing why I didn't want him to come over. "You sure?"

"I'll be fine. I'll be right over."

"Ok, just be careful."

I left the bathroom and quietly covered my nakedness with a pair of jeans and a t-shirt. I slipped on a pair of flats and eyed Wasif, who was still fast asleep. In the den, I grabbed my keys and then slipped out into the garage. I'd nearly made it Corey's when my cell phone rang. At first I panicked, but then I saw that it was Corey.

"You ok? Where are you?" he asked before I could say "hello."

"I'm fine. I'm pulling up to your place now."

I parked my vehicle next to Corey's truck. Corey lived in an old cement factory with towers that had been converted into three-story apartments. Each apartment had balconies on the second and third floors and a rooftop patio.

Corey opened his front door and waited for me to exit my car. I followed him into his living room and sat down on the sofa next to him. The room was almost completely dark except for the dim track lighting that lined the ceiling. I could see well enough to note that the room was minimally decorated. There was a decent-looking beige couch and a blue arm chair. The top of the simple oak coffee table was almost completely covered with issues of *Sports Illustrated* and *ESPN* magazines. It reminded me of his dorm room back in college. It was a pretty impersonal space. A photo of Corey's parents on the matching end table and his name on the magazine labels were the only indications that the apartment belonged to him. It was as if he had no plans to lay down his roots in this place. One would think he was waiting to find a permanent home.

I breathed in the scent of the vanilla air fresher that was plugged into the socket on the wall. The flat screen TV sitting in the corner was tuned to CNN. Corey pressed the mute button on the remote control and then fixed his drowsy eyes on me.

"Tell me," he said softly. I took a deep breath and then began to describe the dream to him.

After listening intently, he said, "You never told me about that."

I nodded. "I know...I was ashamed."

"Of what?"

"There's something about that night that wasn't in the dream. Something else that I remember now."

He nodded. "Ok..."

"When I woke up that night, my underwear was off. I'd been wearing underwear when I fell asleep, but it was gone when I woke up. And...and I was bleeding, and it hurt so bad. He...he raped me, Corey. Before that night, I was a virgin. He *took* that from me. I don't remember all of it, but I know it happened..." My voice broke as I began to sob.

Corey pulled me to him. "Mona, I'm sorry. I'm so, so sorry."

I sniffled and closed my eyes. I rested in his strong arms. Corey had always made me feel so safe, and that night was no different.

"I wish I could meet Quan. I wish I could make him pay for what he did to you." His voice was quivering.

He held me tightly for a long while. I soaked up his consolation. I needed it. I needed *him*.

My tears finally ended, and Corey kissed my forehead before releasing me. "Come with me," he said as he stood and took my hand. I followed him as he climbed the winding stairs to the second, then the third floor, where we climbed another set of stairs to the roof. He opened the door and led me to one of the two white lounge chairs that were sitting side by side on his patio. They almost glowed against the darkness of the night. It was chilly, and when he noticed me rubbing my arms, he ducked back into his apartment and came back out with a blanket. He covered me with it and sat down in the other lounge chair.

He reached over and took my hand in his. "Look up," he said softly. I looked up at the dark sky, dotted with small stars. The moon was full and bright. I almost felt that if I reached up high enough, I could touch it.

"Beautiful, isn't it?" Corey said.

I nodded. "It truly is."

He squeezed my hand. "Whenever life starts to overwhelm me, I come up here. Psalm 33:6 says, 'By the Word of the Lord, the heavens were made, their starry host by the breath of His mouth.' Just by His Word, all of it was created! He's so much bigger than any problem I could ever have. He can fix anything, Mona-Lisa. He can heal any wound."

I felt a tear trickle down my cheek. "I thought I *was* healed, Corey. For years, I never even thought about the things of my past."

Corey reached over and wiped the tear from my cheek. "You didn't let yourself heal. You just blocked it all out."

"What am I supposed to do to heal? I don't know what to do, Corey."

"Give it to God. Give it all to Him. The pain, the anger, all of it."

"How?"

"Pray. Pray even when it feels like no one is listening. Pray and forgive. Forgive your mother. Forgive everyone that hurt you."

I nodded. "Will you pray with me?"

Corey smiled. "Of course I will." He took my hand, and we both bowed our heads and closed our eyes. "Dear Lord, we thank you for your love. We thank you for your mercy. Father, we thank you for our lives. Lord, I know that your Word says that you are close to the brokenhearted. Your Word says that by Jesus' stripes, we are healed. Lord, I pray that you touch Mona-Lisa. Heal her and make her whole. Make your love and presence known to her. Bless her to clearly see that she is never alone, because you walk with her. In Jesus' name, amen."

We sat there under the night sky together, my hand in his. I stared up at the sky and out at the lights of our small city. I looked over at Corey. He was looking up at the sky with a slight smile on his face. He looked so handsome in the moonlight. "Corey, what did you mean by life overwhelming you? Don't you have a good life?"

He looked at me and shook his head. "I have a good life, but I'm human. There are some things I wish I had. Some things about my life I wish I could change."

I frowned. "What do you mean?"

He looked me in the eye. "I get lonely. I want a wife...a family. Can't seem to find the right woman."

I stood and then walked over and sat down beside Corey on his lounger. "You'll find someone. You're too good a man not to. Any woman would be lucky to have you."

He shrugged. "Evidently being a good man isn't too popular these days."

I placed my hand over his. "Did I hurt you when we were younger?"

He looked away from me and nodded. "You did, but I got over it."

"Sometimes it's hard for a person to see how special someone is when they're too close to them. Sometimes you have to lose someone before you realize just what they meant to you." I kissed him softly on the lips.

"Are you speaking for yourself, Mona?"

I nodded. "I'm sorry, Corey. I really am. There are so many things I wish I could change. More than you know."

He stared at me for a moment and then cupped my face in his big strong hands and returned my kiss. I melted. At that moment, I wanted nothing more than for Corey to take me into his bedroom...to his bed. It seemed that Corey shared that desire with me. He stood and took my hand, leading me back into the building. We stopped at the third floor, at his bedroom. The covers were disturbed only on one side of his queen-sized bed. There was a dent in the pillow, reminding me that I'd interrupted his sleep. We sat on the bed, and he began kissing my neck. I tugged at his t-shirt, trying to pull it over his head, and in the process, shocked Corey back into reality. Or maybe it was the open Bible on his night stand. Whichever was the case, his lips left my neck, and he stood to his feet.

He shook his head. "What are you doing, Mona? Hell, what am *I* doing? How did we get from a spiritual discussion to this?"

I looked up at him. "I wanna be with you. Don't you wanna be with me?"

He closed his eyes and rubbed the back of his neck with his

hand. "You were with him tonight, weren't you? I can still smell him on you."

My eyes shot to the floor. I had no response for that. What was I doing? I'd just been with Wasif earlier, but I still wanted Corey, and I wanted him bad.

"Is he still in your bed?"

I kept my eyes on the floor and nodded.

He sighed. "Go home, Mona-Lisa."

I looked up at his face. I wanted to beg him to let me stay. I wanted Corey in the worst way. I felt like I needed him and only him at that moment. I couldn't move, and I couldn't speak, so I just sat there.

"Mona, go back home. As long as you're with him, we can't be together. I told you that."

"But I wanna be with *you*," I said weakly. I sounded like a desperate school girl. I felt like one, too.

He closed his eyes and nodded. "I know you do, and I wanna be with you, but you're with him."

I stood and kissed his neck. "But I'm with you right now. Don't you want me at all?"

"M...Mona..."

I lifted his shirt and admired his body. "My God, you are so beautiful! I mean, you are the finest man I've ever laid eyes on. How did you get this fine?" I rubbed my hand slowly across his chest.

"Uh...um, I work out a lot. I like to work out. It relieves stress..." He opened his eyes and looked at me. "M...Mona, Mona, stop." He said the words, but he didn't follow them up with any action.

I kissed the perfect muscles of his chest. "But didn't you say that you wanted me?"

His resolve back, he grabbed my arms and looked me in the eye. "The issue at hand is not what *I* want. You've got a man in your bed, and you're over here ready to crawl into mine. What do *you* want, Mona?"

I smiled. "I told you, silly. I want *you*."

"For what? Just for tonight? And when I want you again, when I *need* you, will I have to take a number and wait until he's had his turn?"

I stared at him.

"You go get that man out of your bed and your life, *permanently*. Then you can have me. I can be all yours, but for that to happen, you have to be all mine. I'm not some toy you can play with, Mona, and I don't like leftovers. Never have." He let me go and left the room. When he returned, he had my purse and keys in his hand. "Good night, Mona. Call me when you make it back home safely. I'll come over and check on you tomorrow."

I snatched my possessions from him. As he escorted me to the door, I said, "Don't bother checking on me." I don't wear rejection well.

He kissed me on the cheek. "It's not a bother. Be careful going home."

I drove home feeling so confused that I nearly passed by my own house. It was 3:00 A.M. when I crawled back into my bed. As soon as my head hit the pillow, Wasif pulled me into his arms. "Where've you been?" he asked groggily.

"Went for a drive. Couldn't sleep."

He accepted my excuse without any further discussion. As I lay there in his arms, I wished they were Corey's arms.

◆◆◆

Wasif took the boys to school the next morning, and I stayed in bed. I didn't feel all that well, so when I heard a knock at the door, it took all I had in me to drag out of bed, pull on a robe, and answer it. I walked slowly to the door, clutching my queasy stomach.

"Who is it?!" I called.

"Corey."

Great. I sighed and opened the door. I was still a little miffed with him despite the fact that I had no right to be. He'd been right. It was absurd for me to expect him to sleep with me just hours after I'd slept with Wasif, but at that moment, all I'd cared about was fulfilling a need. At that moment, I'd needed Corey. "Corey, I told you that you didn't have to come over. What is it? You didn't reject me enough last night?"

He shook his head. "Good morning to you, too. And I wasn't rejecting *you*, Mona. I was rejecting the situation. Hey, you don't look so good."

I rolled my eyes. "Gee, thanks. I think I'm coming down with something. You better leave. You might catch it."

He smiled. "I never get sick, remember? You need me to get you anything?"

"I think we've got some ginger ale. That always helps. I'll be ok, rea—" before I could finish the statement, I felt a retching feeling in my throat. I turned and ran to the bathroom and, clutching the toilet bowl, heaved until my stomach was empty.

"You alright?" Corey asked from the bathroom doorway.

I shook my head. "I guess not." I stood and splashed cold water from the sink on my face.

"When did you start feeling sick?"

"This morning. Probably some 24-hour bug. I'll be alright."

"I'll stick around for a while. No one should have to be alone when they're sick."

I smiled at him. He really was a great guy and a wonderful friend even though he'd turned down my advances. "What about work?" I grabbed my toothbrush. I had to get that taste out of my mouth.

He shrugged. "I took off. Didn't get much sleep last night."

I shook my head. "I'm sorry for waking you up, Corey," I said, with a mouth full of toothpaste.

"It's ok. Why don't you lie down? I'll be here if you need me."

I wasn't in any condition to argue any further, so after I'd brushed my teeth, I climbed back into bed. After he'd poured me a glass of ginger ale, Corey sat in a chair next to the bed and watched me sleep. When I woke up a little after noon, I smiled at the sight of Corey sitting in the chair with Lizzie sitting in his lap contently. "She likes you," I said groggily.

He shrugged. "I fed her. That seems to go a long way with a dog."

I scooted up in the bed until my back rested against the headboard. "Thank you."

"Nice room," he said.

"Thanks." My bedroom was bathed in white from the walls to the carpet to the bedding. A huge bamboo rug covered most of the carpet. There were bamboo shades on the windows. Bamboo beach mats hung from the walls. I'd hung a chime of seashells from the white ceiling fan. Huge potted palm trees stood in each corner of the room. Floor-to-ceiling book shelves were built into the wall opposite my bed. They were chocked full of books, most of which I'd read from cover to cover. I called that room my paradise. It was my own serene space.

He sat in silence for a moment. Then he sighed and said, "So this is where the magic happens, huh?"

I shook my head. "*Corey...*"

"Ok...ok, I'm sorry. That was out of line. I just need to know why you're doing this. *Why*, Mona? I mean, what do the two of you even have in common besides what happens in that bed?"

"He's the father of my sons, Corey."

"That's it? You have a relationship based on sex and an unplanned pregnancy?"

"He's good to us."

"And that gives him the right to use you?"

"He's never used me. We have an equally beneficial relationship. We're both getting what we want out of it."

He scoffed. "Really? So how does this work? He comes over here and plays house one or two days a week and then runs back home to wifey? And in exchange, you get to live the good life, huh?"

I sighed. "You have no right to judge me, Corey."

He shrugged. "I'm not judging you, Mona. I just want to know how it feels to sell your soul for a house and a car."

I sat up on the side of the bed and looked him in the eye. No matter how fine he was, he was barking up the wrong tree with me. Lizzie hopped out of his lap and onto the bed next to me as if she was switching sides in the middle of a battle. "Well, if you wanna take it there then don't forget about the bank account, the credit cards, and the clothes," I said.

He reached over and tugged at the lace trim lining the bottom of my short black nighty. "He buy this for you? He likes for you to play dress up for him?"

I stared at him and shook my head. "No, actually, he prefers me naked."

He nodded. "And you give him whatever he wants whenever he wants it, huh?"

I raised an eyebrow. "Always and without hesitation. He

gives me what I want, and I give him what he wants."

He laughed bitterly. "Oh, so you're just a simple whore then. You've done all this stuff to escape your past, and you're basically just reliving it. Like mother like daughter, huh? I remember you said those men would give her money and pay her bills. You're doing the same thing. You hated her so much that you've become her."

He'd hit the wrong nerve. I lunged for him and tried to slap him. He caught my wrist and held onto it with little effort. I tried to pull away but couldn't. He stood and brought his face so close to mine that our noses touched. "I'm nothing like that woman, and you know it! Let me go!" I yelled. Lizzie yelped her support from behind me.

He pulled me closer to him and pressed his lips to mine. I pushed against him for a second and then gave in. Well, like I said, he was a good kisser. It was hard for me to resist. Plus, I still wanted him. And let's not forget that the man is super-duper fine.

He finally let go of my wrist and grabbed the back of my gown, gripping it tightly in his hands. I wrapped my arms around him and pulled him closer. We kissed for a long while. When Corey finally let me go, I rubbed my finger across my lips.

"You *think* you want him. You think you want this life, but you want better."

"You can say what you want about Wasif, but he's never called me a whore."

He nodded slowly. "No, he just treats you like one."

I rolled my eyes. "If you say so. Look, my life works for me, Corey. You wouldn't understand. I don't expect you to."

"Oh, it's working, huh? Ok, then why am I here instead of him? Why is it me you confide in and not him? Why did you want me so badly last night? You want me right now, don't you?"

I dropped my eyes. "I don't know. It's complicated. I'm confused."

"Do you love me, Mona-Lisa?"

"I…I don't know."

"Do you love Wasif?"

"I don't know that anymore either."

"But if he climbs back into this bed, he can have you, right?"

I didn't answer.

"And if I climbed into that bed right now, I could have you too, right?"

"I told you, I'm confused. I just want what's best for my

sons. I want them to have better than I had. They have everything they need. That's all that matters to me."

Corey nodded. "Everything except a real father."

"Wasif's a good father, Corey."

"Mona, do you really think this arrangement that you and Wasif have is not affecting those boys? They're old enough to realize things aren't exactly right. They've had to watch their father disrespect their mother for years. How do you think they feel about that?"

"They adore Wasif. And he's never disrespected me, *ever*."

Corey gave a shocked look. "Mona, he married another woman! I could understand things a little better if he'd been married when you met him, but no, he married someone else *after* you had the boys. And you just accepted it and kept giving yourself to him. Why would you do that?"

I felt tears sting my eyes. "Corey, I grew up with nothing. Nothing!"

He held up his hand. "Mona —"

"Sometimes I didn't even have the basic necessities like food, and when I did have food, I had to fight the roaches for it. I did what I had to do to make sure my boys never know what that feels like."

"Mona, I —"

"And I hope you didn't come over here to make me feel bad about that, because I don't. I'll do anything for them, *anything*, including laying down my life if I have to. I'm not perfect, and I haven't always made the best decisions, but I love my sons."

"Mona, I know—"

"Furthermore, I don't have to answer to you. I don't owe you any explanation for the way I've lived my life, and you can go straight to hell if you don't like it!"

The tears flowed freely. I fell back onto the bed and covered my face with my hands. I felt Corey climb into the bed beside me. He pulled me to him, and as mad as I was at him, I still didn't resist. I knew that he'd spoken the truth, but it hurt to hear it. I'd turned my back on the truth years ago. Corey had just made me face it again.

"I'm sorry, Mona. Don't cry," he said softly into my ear.

I continued to sob, burying my face in his chest. He hugged me tightly. "I'm so sorry, baby. I really am. I shouldn't have said that stuff. I just think you deserve better. I care about you, Mona. More than you know," he said.

"Are you what's better, Corey? Is that what you're saying?" I asked through my sobs.

Corey rubbed my back. "All I can say is that I never would've mistreated you. I would've made you my wife, not my mistress."

I nodded. "I know."

We lay there together until we both dozed off. I could've lain there forever, but I woke up when I felt him climb out of the bed.

"Where are you going?" I asked. I really wanted him to stay with me.

He shook his head. "That bed. I can't…"

I wanted to jump up and take him to the guest bedroom, but instead, I said, "Corey, I don't want you to leave."

He rubbed his forehead. "Mona, I don't know what I'm doing anymore. Being near you is making me lose my head. I'm saying crazy stuff. I'm doing crazy stuff. I'm about to do something that is against my better judgment when I know better. I just can't think straight."

I felt tears welling in my eyes again. "I feel the same way. It's like you stepped back into my life and shook up my world. Everything that felt right doesn't feel right anymore. Being with you feels right. That much I know. Please stay. We can go to another room, or we can leave here. I just wanna be near you."

He reached down and rubbed my cheek. "I need to clear my head, Mona. I need to figure out what's going on between us."

I nodded.

"Look, I'mma go and get the boys. We can talk more when I get back. Ok, baby?"

I nodded and smiled. *Baby.* "Ok."

Corey turned to leave my bedroom, but before he reached the door, Wasif walked in with the boys trailing behind him.

Chapter 16

"It's Been You"

Lizzie hopped off the bed and ran to Wasif. She stood at his feet barking, as if filling him in on what had transpired between me and Corey. Wasif ignored her. Evidently he forgot that his sons were standing behind him, or maybe he just didn't care, because the first thing out of his mouth when he saw Corey standing next to the bed was, "What the hell are you doing in here?!"

Morgan and Blair both wore expressions that were a mixture of surprise and confusion.

Corey shrugged. "Mona's been sick. I was just looking after her."

Wasif bucked his eyes. "Looking after her? I think that's *my* job."

Corey nodded. "Yeah, well, you weren't here, so I took care of things," Corey said, sounding less than enthused. I half-expected him to let out a yawn to emphasize his boredom with Wasif.

"What exactly did you take care of?! This is *my* woman, Corey. She's mine! I'm sorry if you couldn't hold on to her, but she's mine now and has been for years! You need to stay away from her."

"You make her sound like a puppy or something. She doesn't belong to anyone except God," Corey said calmly. His calm seemed to fuel Wasif's anger.

"I've had it with you! I'm sick of you lurking around my family. *My family!* Go get one of your own."

I looked at the boys who were watching the exchange intently. I knew that as much as they liked Corey, they wouldn't hesitate to defend their father if they thought they needed to. Especially Morgan. I definitely didn't want Morgan to fight Corey. "Boys, go to your rooms," I said as I sat up on the side of the bed and wrapped the sheet around me.

Neither of them moved a muscle but continued to stare at the two men. "*Now*, boys!" I said.

Finally, they backed out of the room. I walked over to the door and shut it. "Wasif, you're way out of line here," I said.

"Out of line? You have this man in our bedroom, Mo.

You're sitting there in your nightgown, and he's in here leering at your body. The body that belongs to *me*. And *I'm* the one who's out of line?"

"Really, man. You're making her sound like a car or something. That's really not cool," Corey interjected.

I shot Corey a pleading look and then turned to Wasif. "He was helping me. He was even going to pick the boys up for me."

"Speaking of that, why haven't you answered the phone? I was trying to tell you I was gonna pick the boys up."

I frowned. "I don't know, maybe I left the ringer off. Wasif, Corey's been a good friend to me. You should apologize to him."

"He's *your* friend, not mine. I'm not apologizing. He just better get the hell outta here." He turned and left the room.

I grabbed Corey's hand. "I'm sorry, Corey. I really am."

Corey pulled his hand away. "It's alright. He's scared he'll lose you because of the way he got you, and he should be."

"What?"

"Mona, when are you gonna stop treating him like he's your everything when you're obviously not *his* everything."

"Corey, I don't think—"

"I know you don't. You don't think at all, do you? You

don't think about the fact that I'm the one you call when you need to talk. It's my shoulder you cry on. What does he do for you, Mona? And I'm not talking about this house and the money. What is he to you? Better yet, what am I to you?"

I stood and stared at Corey with my mouth hung open, speechless. Corey leaned over and kissed me, taking full advantage of the posture of my mouth. I kissed him back. Part of me hoped that Wasif didn't catch us and another part didn't care if he did.

When his lips left mine, he was smiling. "No answer? That's what I thought. Look, I've been down this road with you before, Mona. Wasif gets all of the pleasure, and I get all of the pain. I'm not doing this again, no matter how much I love you." Corey left my bedroom, and I sat back down on the bed. I'd never meant to hurt him or use him. I cared about Corey, and he'd said that he loved me. *He loves me.*

Wasif walked back into the room with a satisfied look on his face. "He's gone."

"I know. He's my friend, Wasif. *My only friend.* You shouldn't have said that stuff to him, especially not in front of the boys."

"I told the boys it was just a misunderstanding, but you need to stay away from him. *I'm* your friend. I'm the only friend you need. Anything you can tell Corey Sanders, you can tell me."

No I can't. I sighed. "My world can't only consist of you and the kids, Wasif. That can't be healthy."

Wasif put his hands on my shoulders. "You've done fine with it up to now. I don't have any friends either, Mo. All we need is each other. You need to stop letting Corey Sanders tear up our family. Can't you see he's doing this on purposes, Mo? Probably some elaborate plot for revenge."

I shook my head. "He's a good person, Wasif. He wouldn't do something like that."

"He's got you fooled. You wanna see the best in him and ignore the worst. We are all we need. Our family is all we need." He pulled me into a hug, and I closed my eyes.

Wasif stayed home with me that night, and for the first time, I wished he hadn't. As I lay awake in his arms, I came to a realization. While most people can't tell you exactly when they knew they were in love with someone, I'm fortunate in that I can. At that very moment, I knew that I loved Corey. I wanted nothing more than to hear his voice and see his smile. I loved Corey Sanders, but I had no idea what to do about it.

I woke up the next morning determined to sort things out with Corey, but as it turns out, my sickness returned. I ended up spending the morning in bed. By that afternoon, I felt well enough to pick the boys up. After I made it to the school, I went straight to the gym and watched the boys practice. Once they were finished, I followed Corey to his office.

He heard me trotting behind him, trying to catch up. "What is it, Mona?" he said without even bothering to turn around.

"Can we talk?"

He grabbed the doorknob then turned and looked at me. "About what?"

"Us?"

He sighed as he opened the door. He stepped inside and waited for me to follow him. He offered me a seat across from his desk. "You been sick again? You don't look good," he said. *Well, at least he's concerned about me.*

"I'm better now."

He nodded then sat down in the chair behind his desk. "What's going on, Mona?"

"I'm sorry, Corey. I'm sorry about the way Wasif acted."

He shrugged. "Wasif isn't my concern."

"Well, am I your concern? Do you still care about me?"

He looked me in the eye. "Mona, where are you going with

this?"

"Corey, I care about you. I don't wanna lose what we have."

"What do we have, Mona?"

I dropped my eyes. "I...I don't know."

"Then how do you know that you don't wanna lose it?"

"I..." I stared at him and tried to figure out what to say.

"Look, Mona. I'm not for playing games with you. I'm not gonna sneak around behind some married man's back to be with you. Do I care for you? Yes. Do I want to be with you? Yes. But I'm not going to lose my dignity for you again."

I shook my head. "This is not like college. What happened then is different. Back then, you were really a good friend to me, but in my mind, it was nothing more than that. I cared about you, but I wasn't in love with you. There was a spark between me and Wasif from the time I met him. I couldn't resist him."

Corey rolled his eyes and shook his head. "Do I really have to listen to this? He was irresistible, huh? And now?"

"Now, things have changed."

"How?"

I stood and walked over to his desk. I slid onto his lap and could see the excitement in his eyes though he tried to keep his composure. I wrapped my arms around his thick neck and nibbled at his ear. I could smell the remnants of his cologne mixed with the scent of cocoa butter. I turned my head and slowly kissed him on the lips. At first, he didn't kiss me back, but it didn't take long for him to lose his resolve. He cupped my face in his hands and returned my kiss deeply. Once the kiss ended, I stepped back and smiled at him. "Now, it's you that I can't resist."

He was breathing heavily as he said, "You love me, Mona?"

I nodded. "I do."

"You sure this isn't just lust? Cause this attraction between us is crazy. Maybe you just *think* you love me."

I shook my head. "I can't lie, Corey. I want you, but I *know* I love you."

"Does this mean you're gonna stop being Tariq's mistress?" he asked softly.

"Wasif."

"Whatever."

"You've gotta give me some time, Corey. Wasif's not good with conflict. I don't want him to do anything stupid."

Corey frowned. "What do you think he'd do? Take the boys out of the country or something?"

I shook my head. "No, Wasif's totally Americanized. He

was born here, and I don't think he's been to Pakistan more than once in his entire life. He didn't like it all that well."

"Would he hurt you?" The look in his eye changed from one of concern to one of anger. "He thinks you're his property, but I promise he'd better not lay a hand on you, Mona. I can't be responsible for what I might do to him if he hurts you."

I placed my hand on his arm. "He wouldn't do that."

He stared at me, his expression unchanged.

"I've known him a long time. I know he wouldn't do that."

He relaxed. "Well, what then?"

"I don't know, but he's always been afraid of losing our little family. I'm not sure what he'll do to try and hold on to us. Plus, I've never worked. That's his house, his car. They're both in my name, but I don't know what he'll try to pull. I've got a lot to figure out. But, you're who I want, Corey, and I'm not talking friends. I want to *be* with you. Can you just give me time to work things out?"

He shook his head. "I don't know…"

I grasped his hands in mine. "*Please*, Corey. I love you. I can't lose you."

He dropped his eyes. "Mona…"

"Do you want me to beg? I'll beg. I'll get on my knees. Whatever it takes."

He shook his head and then stood and took me into his arms. "I don't want you to beg. I just want to believe you. I want to believe that you'll cut things off with him."

"I will. I just need time."

"I don't have a lot of money, Mona, but I love you. I really do."

I smiled. "Does this mean you'll wait for me?"

He lowered his head and brushed his lips across mine. "I'll wait. I love you. What choice do I have?"

Chapter 17

"You Belong To Me"

The next couple of weeks, I worked hard to keep my word to Corey. I attended church every week with him and the boys. I had lunch with him just about every day, and my dreams started to taper off. And after a week of on-and-off sickness, I was feeling much better. I'd been job hunting, and thanks to some help from Corey, I had an interview at the local library. Things were looking up. The only problem that lingered was Wasif.

I had begun to slowly distance myself from Wasif, but the more I distanced myself from him, the closer he drew to me. For every action there is an equal and opposite reaction, right? Wasif must've aced physics because it seemed that he'd committed Newton's Third Law to memory. Things had gotten to the point where I expected him to leave his wife and move in with me and the boys any second. Suddenly, the one thing I had dreamed of for so long became the one thing I dreaded. I had to end things with him before they went too far. Once Wasif moved into that house, I'd catch hell getting him out.

I finally got up the nerve to tell Wasif my feelings on a Monday, our regular family day, since that was the only day I was sure to see him. Corey had agreed to let the boys spend the night at his apartment, so I waited alone for Wasif. Around 5:00 P.M., he arrived as he usually did, with a big smile on his face and a bouquet of flowers in his hand. "Hey, babe," he said brightly as he leaned over to kiss me. I shrunk away from him. "What's wrong?" he asked.

"We need to talk," I said. I'd prayed for the right words, and Corey had prayed with me several times. I hoped that they would come to me.

He nodded. "Ok, let me see the boys first."

"They're not here."

He frowned. "Ok, let's go in the den."

We both walked into the den. Wasif reached for my hand, but I kept it down at my side. He waited until I sat on the sofa and then sat down so close to me that I could feel the heat from his body. "Mo, what's going on? I mean, you've been acting strange lately, but you're just being weird today."

I took a deep breath and looked him in the eye. Wasif was a beautiful man, and I'd loved him for a long time, but it was time to move on. "Wasif, I want this to end between us. You can see the boys whenever you like, but there can be no more me and you," I blurted.

He stared at me for a moment and then smiled. "This is a joke, right?"

I shook my head. "I'm dead serious. I don't want this life anymore."

"Let me get this straight, Mo. You don't want to live in a big house and have access to all of my credit cards? You don't wanna buy all those fancy clothes and take your poodle to the groomer's on my dime? You don't want to live good and only have to love me in return? *That's* what you don't want anymore?"

I sighed. "Wasif, I do love you, but I can't be your mistress anymore. I deserve better and so do the boys."

"Ok...ok. If this is an ultimatum, I told you I'm gonna leave my wife, but you have to give me time, Mo. *I'm gonna leave*, I promise. Have I ever broken a promise to you before?"

I shook my head. "No, you haven't, but the thing is, I don't care anymore whether or not you leave her. My feelings for you have changed."

"There's someone else? Corey Sanders?"

I looked away from him and didn't answer, but my silence spoke volumes.

"Really? I knew it! I knew he'd worm his way back into your heart somehow," he scoffed. "First you leave him for me, and now you leave me for him. What kinda game is this? Tag, you're it?"

"I'm not playing any games, Wasif. I love him. Maybe I always have."

"Have you slept with him, Mo?"

I sighed. "No, but what right would you have to be upset with me if I had? I'm not your wife, Wasif. And you don't own me."

He shook his head. "That's Corey Sanders talking, not you. You let him get in your head, Mo. We were fine until he came along."

"No we weren't. *You* were fine. You had it all. A wife that would never challenge you and a mistress who was always available for your use."

He frowned. "I've never used you, Mo. I love you."

"Look, Wasif, the point is that you and me are over. No great debate or discussion is gonna change that."

He shook his head. "No, we're not. We're not over."

I bucked my eyes. "Yes, we are. You can't *make* me stay with you."

He looked me in the eye and smiled again. "Does he know that you're pregnant?"

"What the hell are you talking about, Wasif? I'm not pregnant."

"I can't believe you haven't realized it yet. I knew when you started having morning sickness."

I shook my head. "No, I can't be..."

"Did you ever start back on your birth control, Mo?"

"You said I had time, and I guess I just forgot about it. I had so much on my mind..." My voice trailed off as the realization of what was going on set in.

"That's right. You ran out of birth control, and we've been together tons of times since. You're pregnant."

I covered my mouth with my hands and felt the tears as they filled my eyes. At that moment, I fully realized that he was most likely correct. "You did this on purpose, didn't you? You did this because of Corey. You've been acting different ever since he came back into my life. You were *trying* to get me pregnant. How could you do this knowing what a hard time I had carrying the twins?"

"Turns out that I had good reason to be concerned about

you and Corey Sanders, didn't I?"

I closed my eyes and shook my head. *What a mess I'm in.*

He shrugged. "Look, maybe I was trying to get you pregnant, and maybe I wasn't. The fact is that I did." He kneeled down beside me and took my hand from my mouth.

"This changes everything, doesn't it?"

I looked at him as the tears trickled down my cheek. I nodded.

"So, you're gonna stop all this nonsense about leaving me and go cook dinner, right?"

I closed my eyes and nodded again.

"Good. How about some chicken enchiladas? Tomorrow, we can start shopping for baby stuff. You've got to be about four weeks along by now. I hope it's another boy. Maybe we can name him after my father…"

Filled with despair, I tried to tune Wasif out. I couldn't bear to listen to him plan a future that I didn't even want to have with him. I stood and made my way to the kitchen. Wasif followed me. "Hey babe, where are the boys?"

I wiped my cheek and turned to look at him. "At Corey's. They were gonna spend the night with him tonight."

He laughed. "Good, let him babysit," he said. He pulled me into his arms and kissed my neck. "That way we can celebrate our new baby all night long, and I don't have to worry about being quiet. I can teach you some more words in Punjabi as loudly as I want to."

I stiffened against him.

He rubbed my arms as he whispered in my ear. "Relax, babe. I love you. You know that, right?"

"I think you *believe* that you love me."

He smiled eerily. "Mo, I want you to listen to me," he said into my ear. "You stay away from Corey Sanders, you understand? I mean it. We'll just act like you never mentioned leaving me, and everything will go back to normal." *Normal.*

That night I must've cried the entire night. Wasif held me so tightly that I could barely breathe. I lay there and watched my cell phone vibrate against the night stand over and over again. I knew it was Corey. I knew he wanted to know what had happened. I couldn't face him. *Not yet.* I closed my eyes and found no sleep. I lay awake until the night dawned into morning, my heart breaking.

◆◆◆

The next morning, I woke up early and bought three home

pregnancy tests. After reading the results ten times, trying to will the positive signs to turn into negative ones, I drove to Corey's apartment to pick up the boys. With every second of the drive, the crack in my heart grew deeper and deeper. I scolded myself for being dumb enough to believe I was safe without the birth control and for opening my legs every time Wasif appeared. I was in a mess, and it was all my fault. What choice did I have now? There would be another mouth to feed. I couldn't ask Corey to shoulder that kind of responsibility. I had to stay with Wasif. There was no other way.

I knocked on Corey's door and held my breath as I waited for him to answer. Finally, he swung it open without inquiring as to who was on the other side. He knew it was me and from the look in his eye, he knew what I was going to say. He stepped back into the apartment and let me in without saying a word. He wore khaki pants but no shirt, indicating that I'd caught him in the middle of dressing for work. All I could think was, *Lord have mercy.* He pulled me into his arms and kissed me so deeply, I nearly fell. He finished the kiss and then picked up his navy blue polo shirt from the sofa and pulled it over his head.

"Where are Blair and Morgan?" I asked.

"Their father came and picked them up a little while ago. He was happy to tell me how you two had reconciled. He told me to stay away from you. That we'd never be together. Tell me he was lying, Mona. Please tell me what he said isn't true."

I shook my head. "Corey, I'm sorry."

He backed away from me. "Damn, Mona. You're sorry? So it's true? You're staying with him?"

I nodded and blinked back tears. "Yes."

He threw up his hands and laughed bitterly. "I shoulda known that my love wouldn't be enough for you to give up the life he's given you." I reached for his hand. He snatched it away from me. I felt tears roll down my cheek.

"That's not it, Corey. That's not it at all."

"Then what the hell are you doing? What is it?"

I fiddled with my car keys and stared at the floor. I was so ashamed of myself that I couldn't look him in the face. "I love you, but m…my circumstances have changed. I'm surprised Wasif didn't tell you that I'm—"

He held up his hand. "You *love* me? You love *me*, but you're staying with *him*? I don't want to hear anymore. I don't wanna hear whatever lies he told you to pacify you. I don't wanna hear about your mixed up loyalties to him or your love for him, or what you think is right for those boys. Those boys need a real family, Mona, and a real father. It's not fair to them to have to be a part of this sick game you and Wasif are playing."

"Corey, listen. There are some things that you should know—"

"No, Mona-Lisa, *you* listen. I'm done. I don't know why I believed you'd leave him. I've opened my heart to you two too many times, and things always end the same. You love him so much? Then go be with him! Leave me the hell alone, Mona! Go on with your life, and I'll go on with mine. Don't call me. Don't come by. Hell, don't even wave at me in a crowd." He gripped my arm and ushered me to the door.

He hesitated and then leaned in and kissed me hard this time. I nearly fell backward. "That was a goodbye kiss. I want you to know what you're missing out on. I want you to want me and know that you'll never have me. I want you to know exactly how I feel." He shut the door in my face. I cried all the way back home.

Chapter 18

"Ain't No Need to Worry"

"**Get** *your tail up and wash them dishes, Mo!" my mother* shrieked.

Startled from a sound sleep, I bolted up in the bed. I looked at Cleo's side and remembered that she was gone. It'd been three *months since I'd seen my little sister, and I missed her terribly.* "Ma'am? What time is it?" I asked groggily.

"Don't matter. Me and Black hungry and ain't no dishes clean," she said through a puff of cigarette smoke. Black was her boyfriend for that moment.

I squinted at the clock on the wall. It was 2:00 A.M. "I washed them before I went to bed. Everything was clean." I looked at my mother who was wearing a short t-shirt and panties.

"Well, it ain't clean now. Get up and wash them."

I hated my mother, I was tired of her crap, I was upset about my sister disappearing and at sixteen, I had enough hormones to share with most of the female population at my school. So suffice it to say that I wasn't in the mood for my mother's mess. So I simply said, "No."

My mother bucked her eyes at me. "The hell you say to me, girl?!"

"I got school in the morning. I'm not getting up to wash no dishes." *You and Black can eat off the damn floor if you want to,* I thought.

"Who you talking to like that? I said get up and wash them dishes!!"

I rolled my eyes. "And I said no."

I saw her hand coming toward my face, and I ducked. She lost her balance and fell onto the bed. I hopped up. She glared up at me and stood in front of me, nose to nose. We were both breathing heavily, and my adrenaline was off the charts. I was in fight or flight mode and fight was my action of choice.

"Mo, I don't know if you're smelling yourself or what, but you gone make me kick you're tail up in here tonight."

I stared straight into her eyes. "You can try, but I ain't no little girl no more." *Game on.*

She lunged for me, and we wrestled and fought for a long while, yelling and screaming at each other. She wore out quicker than I did, thanks to her nicotine addiction, and her fight became more noise *than anything. Fueled by my pure loathing for her, I fought on, pulling her hair and scratching her face. I honestly believe that if her boyfriend hadn't gotten in between us, I might've killed my mother. I can't say that I would've regretted it.*

"Ay! Y'all cut that junk out!" Black yelled as he pulled my mother away from me. Standing there in nothing but his black boxer briefs, he disgusted me as much as my mother did. "What's going on?" he asked.

Breathing heavily, my mother said, "I was trying to get this little heifer to wash dishes so I could fix us something to eat, and she gone start a fight with me."

"Well damn baby, you wash 'em. The girl was sleep. I'da prolly tried to kick yo' tail if you woke me up talking 'bout some dishes. That's just stupid." Suddenly, I liked Black a whole lot more than I had before.

Mama glared at me and then left my room. Black left right behind her. I settled back into bed with a smile on my face. That was the last time my mother mistreated me. Maybe if I'd stood up to her earlier, Cleo wouldn't have left.

I sat up in the bed, and I must've startled Wasif. He sat up, too. "What's going on, babe? What happened?" he asked, half-asleep and half-awake.

I looked at him. "I had a dream. A bad dream."

He patted my arm and lay back down. "Oh. Well, go back to sleep."

"Wasif?"

"Yeah, babe."

"Can I tell you about my dream?"

Silence.

"Wasif?"

In the darkness, I could hear his soft snore. He'd gone back to sleep.

I lay back down and stared at my cell phone on the night stand. I picked it up and tipped into the bathroom. I dialed Corey's number and listened as it rang to voicemail. I hung up without leaving a message. I sat on the toilet and cried.

The next morning when I dropped the boys off at school, I saw Corey on the parking lot, and my heart leaped. When the boys saw him, they jumped out of the car and headed in his direction. I watched as he greeted them with a smile. I wanted to talk to him. I wanted to be with him. I missed him so much. He looked in the direction of my car and stared for a moment before turning towards the school. Not so much as a wave or even a nod. He hated me, and I can't say that I blamed him. Right about then, I hated myself.

♦♦♦

The day I'd once dreamed of had finally arrived. Wasif had finally left his wife, and I was in total and complete misery. Sundays were my best days. On Sunday, I had two full hours of peace, plus I got to see Corey that entire time. I loved Sundays. I relished them, or at least I did, until...

The boys and I walked into the huge sanctuary and sat in our usual spot. Corey didn't sit with us anymore, but I could count on him sitting somewhere in that same section. I liked to think that he wanted to be near me, too. But that might have been wishful thinking. I had hurt him not once but twice. He was done with me.

I'd settled into my seat when I spotted him. I couldn't take my eyes off of him. He looked gorgeous in a chocolate brown suit and cream shirt. His tie was gold. He was smiling as he took his seat. The boys hopped up and went over to speak to him, blocking my view of him for a moment. When they finally returned to their seats, my stomach dropped. There was a woman sitting next to Corey. She was thin and pretty, and they were having a very lively conversation.

Did Corey have a girlfriend now? I tried to look away but couldn't. I saw her rest her hand over his, and what was left of my heart shattered. I blinked back tears. As the service began, I noticed her whispering in his ear. He leaned over close to her and wrapped his arm around her shoulder as she spoke, then he smiled brightly and nodded. He looked up and saw me and his smile faded. He stared at me for a moment and then nodded his acknowledgement of me. But in my mind, the nod meant, *yeah I'm with her, now.* I finally turned my attention to the service. Or at least I turned my head, because honestly, Corey and the mystery woman never left my mind. I couldn't tell you what the sermon was about. I don't even remember what songs were sung. All I remember is that the man I love was with another woman.

After church, we headed straight home, where Wasif was waiting for us. I quietly cooked dinner and, of course, thought about Corey. By the time dinner was finished, I was more angry than hurt. If Corey was supposed to love me, how could he move on so easily? And how could he flaunt that woman in front of me like that, and in church no less? Now fuming, I left the kitchen, walked into the den, grabbed my purse and keys, and headed out the door. Wasif and the boys were in the den watching a movie, and as I passed them by, they gave me a trio of curious looks.

"Going somewhere?" Wasif asked.

"I need to pick something up," I said and continued out the door without waiting for his response. I backed out of my driveway and headed to Corey's apartment. I wanted to give him a piece of my mind, and I knew he'd just ignore a phone call. So, I decided to do it face to face.

I parked in front of his apartment and quickly walked up to his door and knocked hard. I stood there for a moment, and then I knocked again.

"Coming!" I heard him call from inside. "Who is it?" he asked as he approached the door.

"Mona!" I answered anxiously.

The door swung open, and on the other side stood Corey, just as fine as ever, still in his church clothes. With a shocked look on his face, he said, "Mona? What the —"

I pushed past him and walked into the apartment. "What the hell do you think you're doing?!" I said, my voice trembling.

He closed the door behind me and frowned. "What the hell are you talking about?"

"*That woman*. What the hell were you doing with that woman at church?"

"What?" He seemed genuinely shocked.

"*Who was she*, Corey? And how could you flaunt her in my face like that? Is she here? I bet she's here right now." I left the living room and peeped in the kitchen.

He followed me into the kitchen. "You have lost your mind, haven't you? It's not your business who I spend my time with! Did you forget that you dumped me for your baby daddy? Or has that changed?" He was right, but my feelings were hurt, and I was pregnant. That's not a good recipe for being rational.

I nodded. "Oh, so y'all *spending time* together, huh? Ok. I see. You dirty —"

"Mona! YOU dumped ME! What is wrong with you?!"

I put my finger in his face. "Don't try to change the subject. Don't try to turn this around on me, Corey Lamont Sanders. You said you loved me, and before I can turn my head good, you're grinning all up in some chick's face. I guess you fell out of love pretty quickly, huh?"

Corey shook his head. "Ok, that answers my question. You *have* lost your mind. I'm not having this discussion with you, Mona-Lisa. You have the nerve to come over and act a fool with me over who I'm with? And I bet Khalid is at your house right now. Hell, he's probably in your *bed* right now, and the sad thing about it is that you're probably gonna leave here and jump right in the sack with him. I'mma pray for you and especially for those boys."

"Come on now, you're doing this on purpose. What are you

doing? Picking any random Muslim name? His name is Wasif," I corrected.

"In case you haven't figured this out yet, I don't give a damn what his name is."

He grabbed my arm and steered me to the door, but I wasn't giving up that easily. "You never answered my question, Corey. What's going on with you and that woman?"

Corey opened the front door. "Stop this, Mona. It's not doing either one of us any good."

I stood there and stared at him for a moment. I felt the tears well up in my eyes. "I love you, Corey. Why do you hate me so much?"

Corey sighed and then closed the door. He moved close to me. So close that it was hard for me not to touch him. It was so hard that I actually reached for his face. He grabbed my wrist and stopped me. "I don't hate you, but you made a decision to stay with what's-his-name. I've accepted it and moved on, that's all. What do you want me to do? Curl up in the fetal position and cry over you? I can't do that."

I felt a tear roll down my cheek. "Moved on? What is that supposed to mean?" I nearly whined.

Corey wiped the tear away. His lips nearly touched mine as he said, "It means that I'm living my life, Mona. I suggest that you go ahead and live yours." His voice was soft and almost soothing.

I shook my head. "But I can't live my life until I know if you still love me. Do you?"

He looked me in the eyes and gently caressed my cheek. "You just have to hear me say it, huh? Gotta have things your way."

I nodded.

He held my face in his hands and stared at me for a moment. "You miss me, Mona-Lisa?"

I nodded again.

He leaned in close to my ear and whispered, "I miss you too." Then he softly kissed my cheek. He backed away from me and opened the door then said, "To answer your question, it doesn't matter if I love you or not. It never did. That's the problem." He took my hand and kissed it. "Goodbye, Mona-Lisa."

I hesitated to leave, but I realized I was fighting a losing battle. I finally left his apartment and slowly drove home. I felt like someone had kicked me in the gut. I walked though the house straight to my bedroom and closed and locked the door. I laid in the bed, and cried. I cried and cried, and then I just laid there and stared at the wall. I'd been lying there a few minutes when I heard a knock at the door. "Babe, you ok in there?" Wasif asked through the door.

"I'm fine," I said.

"Well, what's going on with dinner? Me and the boys are hungry."

"It's ready. It was ready before I left."

"Ok. Are you gonna come and fix our plates?"

I stood and walked to the door and yanked it open. "Since when did you break your hands? *You* fix 'em!" I shouted.

He gave me a startled look and then said, "O…ok."

I slammed the door shut in his face and locked it again. I slid to the floor and sat with my back against the door and cried.

Chapter 19

"I Can't Sleep"

I lay in the bed glaring at a sleeping Wasif and trying to figure out why I'd ever loved him so much. Why had I wanted him so badly in the beginning? Besides the fact the he was gorgeous and rich, we had nothing in common. There was no real bond other than the fact that we shared two sons, and that bond was fading quickly. I rolled over and stared at my phone on the nightstand. I wanted to call and apologize to Corey. No, actually I wanted to hop in my car and drive over to his place and make him listen to me as I spilled out my heart to him. I'd had my chance to make things right with him, but I'd wasted that opportunity by behaving like a jealous lunatic. I wasn't mad at him anymore. I just missed him and I loved him.

I closed my eyes and prayed for a dreamless sleep. I'd been having nightmares about my past nearly every night, and it was beginning to take a toll on me. I was tired and stressed out. I lay there awake for awhile, almost afraid to fall asleep, but then exhaustion took over. Before I knew it, I'd fallen into a deep slumber.

In my sleep, memories of my mother's abuse flooded my mind. I recalled the times Cleo and I went to school smelly and dirty because Mama refused to wash our clothes or the times we had no food because she'd sold her food stamps. I remembered the men she paraded in and out of our home, the wild parties, the drugs, and the booze. I remembered Cleo. My former life was haunting me, Cleo was haunting me, and I felt like I'd never have any peace until I found her. Not knowing where she was all these years had left a gaping hole inside of me.

Something inside of me told me that if I found Cleo, my mind could rest. At least then, one problem would be solved. So the next afternoon, a Saturday afternoon, the boys and I rode to Jacksonville, to see my mother.

As I pulled in front of the drab, gray-bricked duplex, my heart began to pound in my chest. I hadn't seen my mother since right after the boys were born. I wasn't afraid of her anymore, but I'd be lying if I said I wasn't afraid of what I might do to her. Fueled by the memories, my disdain for her felt fresh and raw. But I had to find Cleo, and the only place I knew to start was with her.

I turned to the boys. "Stay here and lock the doors. I'll be back." They both nodded in response. I'd told them I was going to visit my mother, but I needed to see how she'd act before I let them meet her. Knowing my mother, she might've come to the door naked.

I walked up to the dirty door that led into apartment B and knocked. I inspected the withered potted plants that sat next to the door while I waited for an answer. "Who is it?!" a voice from inside finally yelled. The voice sounded too weak to be my mother's. Maybe she'd moved.

"Um, I'm looking for Christina Dandridge," I said through the door.

The voice was closer to the door this time. "I didn't ask who you were looking for. I asked who it is."

"My name is Mona-Lisa Dandridge. Christina's my mother."

After a few seconds, I heard the chain on the door rattle, and then it slowly opened. The smell of stale cigarette smoke filled my nose and sank into my gut. My hypersensitive nose was a side-effect of my pregnancy. I held my stomach and inspected the woman who stood on the other side of the door.

She was a little shorter than me. We had the same eyes. She could've been my mother, but she looked much older than my mother.

"Mo?" she said. That's when I saw that familiar glint in her eye. It *was* my mother, but age hadn't been kind to her. Instead of looking her true fifty years of age, she could've easily passed for sixty, maybe even sixty-five. Gone were the shapely legs and wide hips that had made my mother so attractive and so popular with the men. Her fair brown skin was wrinkled, and her hazel eyes were surrounded by dark circles. Her wavy black hair was pulled back into a messy ponytail. She was wearing loose-fitting gray jogging pants and a dingy white t-shirt. Only a shell of the woman who raised me was left.

"Yes. Can I come in?" I said.

She nodded, and I followed her into the living room. The only light in the room was a naked low-wattage bulb that hung from the wood grain ceiling fan, but I could see that not much had changed. She still had that same old beige, floral couch that Cleo and I had slept on when we were kids. The dark shag carpet was worn and so dirty that much of it was slick in appearance. There were the same old farmhouse paintings hanging on the wood-paneled walls. An unfamiliar and unattractive recliner sat in the room. There was a tall can of beer sitting on the floor next to it. Mama took a seat in the recliner, and I sat across from her on the edge of the sofa.

"Mama, you look good," I lied.

She shook her head. "No, I don't. This cancer's kicking my behind."

I frowned. "You have cancer?"

"Lung cancer. It was those durn cigarettes."

"I'm sorry, Mama."

Mama pulled a cigarette from a package sitting on the coffee table and lit it. She took a long drag and then broke into a coughing fit. She shrugged and laughed bitterly. "You gotta die from something."

I nodded and tried to hold my breath. I hated the smell of cigarettes, especially cheap cigarettes.

"So, Mo, what you doing back here? Never thought I'd see you again."

Me either. I clasped my hands together. "I've been thinking about my childhood a lot lately and about Cleo."

Mama took another drag from her cigarette. Another coughing fit. "Um hmm," she grunted.

"Um, I want to find Cleo."

She picked up the beer can and took a long drink from it.

"Good luck," she said sarcastically. "You want a beer?"

I fixed my eyes on a dark spot on the wall and tried to erase the image of choking her out of my head. "No, thank you. Have you heard from her at all? I mean, did she ever write or call after she left?"

She shook her head. "You know me and Cleo wasn't that close. I don't think she was too concerned about staying in touch with me."

"But me and Cleo *were* close. I can't believe that she just up and left without even leaving me a note or something."

Mama stared at me for a moment and then stood and left the room. I watched her frail frame disappear into her bedroom. I heard a man's voice asking her what was going on, and then I heard her say, "Nothing, go back to sleep." Same old Mama. She always had a man in her bed.

She was in there a few minutes before she finally returned to the living room. She sat back down in her chair and tossed a folded piece of notebook paper onto the old Formica coffee table. It must've once been white but was now more beige in color. The blue lines were faded.

I looked up at her. "What's that?"

Through a phlegmy cough, Mama said, "Read it."

My hands trembled as I picked up the paper and unfolded

it. It was Cleo's handwriting. Even at twelve years old, she had beautiful penmanship. My eyes blazed a trail on the paper as I read the words.

I'm going away. Please don't look for me. I'm just tired of being sad and scared all the time. I'm sorry to leave you Mo. You're stronger than me. I know you'll be ok.
Love,
Cleo

I wiped a single tear from my cheek as I folded the paper back up. "You had this all along?" I asked.

"Yeah," Mama said, offering no explanation as to why she'd kept it from me, and I didn't ask.

"Mama, did you ever call the police or report her missing?"

She hesitated and then said, "At first, I thought she'd come back. After a week passed, I called 'em, but they didn't do nothing. Do they ever?"

"No posters or milk cartons or nothing?"

"No. Look, Mo, she probably got out there and got strung out or something. Who knows, maybe she dead by now. She was weak; you were always the strong one." She didn't sound like she cared about Cleo at all. Not even a little.

I shook off her words and said, "Do you have a picture of her that I can have?"

Mama nodded towards a bookshelf in the corner of the room. "There's a photo album over there. You can have the whole thing if you want."

I walked over to the bookshelf and found the photo album lying on top. It was hunter green with gold trim. I blew the dust off of the cover and opened it. There were baby pictures of me and Cleo, a few Polaroid snap shots of us both, and school photos chronicling both of our lives. Cleo's pictures stopped at the sixth grade. Mine went on until my graduation.

I sat down and held the book in my lap. "Do you ever think about her?"

"I try not to."

I nodded. We sat in silence for an excruciatingly long time before Mama spoke again. She leaned forward in her seat with the burning cigarette dangling between her fingers, and out of the blue she said, "If you looking for me to apologize for the things that happened in the past then all I can say is I did the best I knew how to do. My mama wasn't mother of the year, no matter how holy she tried to act. She just used her religion to judge me. I had it way worse than y'all did when I was growing up." I guess that was her version of an apology or something. "Oh, by the way, she dead now. Had a heart attack a couple of years back," she added.

I'd liked my grandmother, and it made me sad to hear that she'd passed away. I wished I could've at least gone to her funeral. "I'm sorry to hear that."

Mama nodded.

Another period of silence.

She leaned forward in her chair. "You married now?"

"No, I'm not married."

"You still with that Indian boy?"

"Yes." There was no need in clarifying Wasif's race with her. To her he'd always been "that Indian boy."

"How are your boys?"

"They're fine. They're outside if you wanna see them."

Mama shrugged. "They can come in."

I stood and walked over to the door. I opened it and beckoned the boys to the duplex. I watched as they lazily walked up the side walk, uncertainty in their eyes.

I closed the door behind us, and the three of us sat on the sofa. "This is Blair, and this is Morgan," I said, pointing each boy out to her. "Boys, this is your grandmother."

They smiled and said, "Hi."

For the first time since I'd stepped foot in that place, Mama smiled. "They some good-looking boys, Mo. That one there don't even look like he's got no black in him. He looks straight Indian," she said, pointing at Blair.

"Pakistani," Blair said softly. I knew he wasn't going to let that error pass.

I half-expected my mother to cuss him out for correcting her, but instead, she smiled and said, "Oh yeah. That's right. Pakistani." I was glad she didn't act a fool with Blair, because I couldn't have been responsible for my actions if she'd said the wrong thing to him.

I smiled. "Yes, Blair looks a lot like his father."

"They gone be some real heartbreakers, if they ain't already. You and that boy shoulda had a bunch of kids if they was gone all look like these two."

I smiled. "Thank you." I didn't bother telling her I was pregnant. I hadn't even worked up the nerve to tell the boys yet.

"They look clean cut, too. You done good, Mo."

"Thank you." Another awkward silence fell upon us, and the boys looked as uncomfortable as I felt. "Well, we better be going," I finally said.

"Ok." Mama walked us to the door. "If you find Cleo, tell her I said hi," Mama said as I climbed into my truck.

"Ok. Bye, Mama."

"Bye, Mo."

As I backed out of the driveway, Blair asked, "Is this where you grew up, Ma?"

I nodded, afraid my voice would break if I spoke.

"And that was really your mom?" Morgan chimed in.

Another nod.

We rode back to Conway in silence. I would've loved to tell Corey about seeing my mom, but I couldn't.

Chapter 20

"Angel"

I sat at the dining room table with Lizzie at my feet, surfing the web, doing a little personal research, and trying to find any sign of my sister. I'd spent most of the day checking all of the social networking sites. Surprisingly, there were several Cleopatra Williams' listed, but none of the pictures matched how I thought Cleo would look at thirty. Maybe I was chasing my own tail. Maybe eighteen years was too long to find anyone. Or maybe Cleo still didn't want to be found. Worst than that, maybe she was dead.

I felt someone standing over my shoulder. I looked up to find Wasif hovering over me. "You need something?" I asked, annoyed. I clicked to a different tab.

"What you researching?" he asked. He studied the screen and then said, "Reading up on fraternal twins? You think you're having twins again?"

"No, I was just reading some stuff."

"Oh, ok. What have you learned?"

I shook my head. "Nothing much."

"Well, I'm thirsty. Can you fix me something to drink?"

"The refrigerator is in the same spot, Wasif. It hasn't moved."

He stood there for a moment, shocked. In the past, I would've been glad to wait on him hand and foot, but this wasn't the past.

"Really, Mo?" he finally said.

I rolled my eyes. "Yeah, *really.*"

He sighed and walked over to the refrigerator. When he finally left the kitchen, I resumed my search.

I checked Searchbug. I searched Google and tried to see if there was even one article about a girl going missing in Jacksonville, Arkansas, eighteen years ago. Nothing. What kind of world is this that allows a little girl to just disappear without a trace? Frustrated, I stood from the table and walked over to the refrigerator. Wasif was back in the den with the boys. I sighed. *May as well get started on dinner.* As I seasoned the steaks, Cleo stayed on my mind. *What would I have done if I were her? Where would I have gone?*

I wrapped the huge potatoes with foil and placed them in

the oven. I slid the steaks onto the lower rack and that's when it hit me. She probably changed her name! If she didn't want to be found, she wouldn't have kept using her real name. *Think, Mo, think. What name would she have used?* I sat back down in front of the computer and wracked my brain. Who was her favorite singer? Michael Jackson. Her favorite cartoon? Scooby Doo. Favorite TV show? Martin. She loved Gina. Gina! That's it.

I typed *Gina Williams, Arkansas* into the search box on Searchbug. With any luck, she'd stayed in Arkansas. There were three hits, including one for a Gina Williams-Grant. One in Camden, one in Fayetteville, and Mrs. Grant was in West Memphis. There were phone numbers for all three. I rushed through the house to my bedroom and grabbed my cell phone. I called the Gina in Camden first. No answer but I left a message with my name and number. If it was Cleo, she'd know it was me.

The Gina in Fayetteville answered, and I could quickly tell that she was a white woman. She confirmed that she wasn't my sister, and I quickly hung up and dialed Gina Williams-Grant's number.

"Hello?" I could tell it was a black woman's voice.

"Hello, is this Gina Williams-Grant?"

She answered with a hesitant, "Yes. Who is this?"

"My name is Mona-Lisa Dandridge. I'm looking for my sister. Her name was Cleo Williams. I was wondering if maybe you knew or heard of her." *Are you her?*

Silence from the other end.

"H...hello? Are you still there?" I asked.

"I don't know a Cleo Williams. I'm sorry I couldn't help you." Then a click.

I laid my phone on the table and looked up at the picture of Cleo I'd framed and hung on my dining room wall next to the pictures of myself, Blair, and Morgan. I sighed. *Maybe I should go on TV or the radio or something,* I thought. I shook my head. *It was a bad idea. I'll never find her. Forget it.* I went back into the kitchen and finished cooking dinner.

◆◆◆

I lay stiff as a board as Wasif plied my body with kisses. He finally reached my lips and kissed them. I didn't kiss him back. My mind was full of a lot of things, but making love to him was not one of them.

He sighed. "You know, Mo. I'm having a good time here. You wanna join me?"

I shook my head and pulled the covers up over my body. "I don't feel like it, Wasif."

"Well, I do. *Come on, Mo.* Why are you making me beg?" he whined.

"Why are you even asking? You're gonna do it anyway. If I go to sleep, you'll just take it."

"Why are you making it sound so bad? You used to love it when I woke you up like that."

"Yeah, well things have changed, Wasif. And I'm tired. I'm pregnant, remember? Not tonight, ok?"

Wasif fell back onto his side of the bed. "I don't understand you, Mo. You wanted me here full time, and I'm here. I left my wife for you. My dad's threatening to buy me out of the practice. What more do you want?"

I sat up in the bed and looked at him. "Don't you act like you did me some favor. I wanted out of this relationship. You decided to get me pregnant on purpose, so deal with it."

"I'm just saying, the least you could do is have sex with me."

"I DON'T WANT TO!!!! *DAMN!!!*" I flung my legs over the side of the bed and grabbed my robe.

He reached for my arm and nearly made my skin crawl. I was beginning to hate him. "Where are you going, Mo?"

"I'll sleep on the couch."

"Wait, come back. I won't bother you. I don't want the boys to wake up and find you on the sofa."

I hesitated and then slid back into the bed. I turned my back to Wasif and stared at my phone lying on the night stand. I missed Corey.

Chapter 21

"Only For a While"

I lay back in the tub until my head rested on the rim. The scent of the chamomile bubble bath filled the steamy bathroom as I closed my eyes and thought about that night on the roof. I pictured the stars and the peaceful look on Corey's face. I felt myself smiling as I thought about his smile. It'd been two months since the day I told him I was staying with Wasif. I rubbed my growing belly and sighed. I hadn't been to church in weeks. I'd fallen back into my normal life with Wasif. The only difference was that I was no longer his mistress. I was his fiancé. He'd filed for divorce and asked me to marry him, and I'd accepted. What else was I supposed to do? I couldn't be with Corey, so what difference did it make if I married Wasif?

I heard the bathroom door open, and I opened my eyes. My smiled widened at the sight of Corey standing in the doorway.

I sat up straight in the tub, so excited to see him that I nearly leaped to my feet. "Corey, what are you doing here?" I asked softly.

He didn't speak but slowly moved towards me. Once he reached the tub, he kneeled beside it and gently caressed my cheek.

"Corey —" I began, but he interrupted me.

"Shh," he said, placing a finger to my lips. He leaned in and kissed me. "Mona," he said. "Mona…Mona…Mo…"

"Mo!"

I nearly jumped out of my skin when I heard Wasif's voice. I opened my eyes and saw Wasif standing in the doorway. It had all been just a dream. I wanted to cry.

"Are you that unhappy to see me?" he asked.

I frowned. I didn't feel like giving him any reassuring lies. "What are you talking about, Wasif?"

"You were smiling when I opened the door. Now you just look miserable."

"I…I was dreaming. And I'm not miserable, I'm pregnant and uncomfortable. That's all."

He nodded.

"Where've you been? Sneaking around my back with your wife?" It was his day off and he'd been gone so long I'd hoped he was gone for good.

He shook his head. "No, she wouldn't allow that."

I raised my eyebrows. "Wow, really?" I scoffed.

He sighed. "I didn't mean —"

I raised a wet hand and said, "Whatever, Wasif."

After a moment of silence he said, "You should be careful about falling asleep in the tub." He hesitated and then added, "Were you dreaming about Corey Sanders? You still have feelings for him?"

Did you think they'd just disappear? I closed my eyes. "I don't wanna talk about that."

"You were saying his name and...and you were moaning."

I didn't open my eyes or respond to him.

"You'll get over him in time. I promise. You'll love me just like you used to. I'll be so good to you that you'll *have* to love me again. You'll see." He turned and left the bathroom, closing the door behind him.

I wrapped my arms around my knees and let my tears flow freely. I loved Corey and I missed him so much that I ached inside.

◆◆◆

I was getting dressed for my doctor's visit when I heard the doorbell. Half of me wished it would be Corey, coming to declare his love for me and demanding that I leave with him, but that wasn't Corey's style, and I knew better, anyway. I'd just buttoned the last button on my blouse when I reached the door. I checked the peep hole and nearly fell backward.

I opened the door. "Dr. Masood, I wasn't expecting you."

Wasif's father nodded and then stepped into the foyer without an invitation. I guess he thought he didn't need one. I closed the door behind him and said, "Is everything alright?" I didn't bother to offer him a seat in the living room. I was sure he didn't plan to stay long.

He straightened his already straight black necktie and cleared his throat. "Well, that's what I'm here to find out." His accent was so thick that one wouldn't believe he'd spent the last forty years of his life in the United States.

I frowned. "What do you mean?" I was playing dumb, but I knew he was referring to Wasif leaving his wife.

He clasped his hands in front of him. "I would like to know what you did or said to influence my son to throw his life and all he's worked for away."

I crossed my arms at my chest. "I'm sure I don't know what you're talking about. Wasif is a grown man. Any decision he's made, he's made on his own."

"Surely you're aware of the hold you have on him. He thinks he cannot live without you, so I accepted your former arrangement. Now, he's left his proper wife and moved in here."

Proper wife. I wanted to say, "*Surely you're aware that you can go to hell,*" but I didn't. Instead, I said, "I didn't ask him to. Like I said, he's a grown man, and he made his own decision." *And I don't even want him here.*

He nodded. "You know, I've always accepted that he doesn't always make the best decisions. When he told me about the twins, I knew that he was young and foolish. But now he tells me that you are with child again." He eyed the small bulge in my belly. "This is true?"

I rubbed my stomach and nodded. "It is."

"And Wasif feels it's his obligation to be here. He has other children, you know."

"I'm well aware of Wasif's other family but not nearly as aware as Wasif is."

Dr. Masood's eyes narrowed. "Other family? What you have here is not a family, young lady. It's a situation. A situation that I hope resolves itself soon."

"Resolves itself? I certainly hope you don't think I'm going to terminate this pregnancy, because if you do then you're sadly mistaken. And whether you like it or not, my sons and I are not just going to disappear. If you have a problem with what Wasif's doing with his life, then you need to talk to him. I don't control his mind."

He looked at me for a moment and then said, "I don't think Wasif is thinking with his mind. I think he's being led by another member of his body. I've heard about the seductive ways of black women, but now I've seen it for myself. You've completely mesmerized my son."

I laughed and shook my head. "Like I said, he's a grown man, a *thirty-five-year-old man*, Dr. Masood. He makes his own decisions. Now if you don't mind, I'd like for you leave now. I've heard enough."

He walked to the door and hesitated in the doorway. "You are a very clever woman, Ms. Dandridge. You've played your hand well. At this rate, Wasif will be taking care of you for the rest of your life."

"You know absolutely nothing about me," I scoffed. Taking a page from Corey's book, I shut the door in his face. I walked back into my bedroom, fuming. Had I still wanted to be with Wasif, I would've called and told him what happened. But I didn't want to be with him. Truth be told, I didn't want another baby by him either, but I didn't believe in abortion, so that was not an option.

I grabbed my keys and purse and turned to head out of the room when I first felt the pain. It was excruciating, almost crippling. I eased down to my bed and sat there for a long while, clutching my purse, before I attempted to stand up again. Wasif had whined and whined until I finally gave in and slept with him the night before. Had something happened to the baby because of that? First the pain, then the blood. I nearly screamed when I saw the blood on my white comforter. I clutched my cell phone, and I dialed Wasif's number.

Straight to voicemail.

Damn! I forgot he was in surgery, but why didn't the nurse answer it? I left a message and tried to figure out what to do next.

I need to get to the doctor's office. I was hunched over as I walked through the house and out to the garage. I climbed into my truck with tears streaming down my face.

So much pain.

I had backed out onto the street when everything went black. That's all I remember.

Chapter 22

"No More Tears"

I slowly opened my eyes, stared at the fluorescent lights above my head, and quickly realized that I was in the hospital. I turned my head and saw a man sitting in a chair in the corner. He was blurry. I squinted in an attempt to make him out.

"She's awake." I recognized Blair's voice behind me.

I rolled over and smiled weakly at both of my sons as they stood next to my bed with eyes full of concern. "H...how'd you get here?" I asked. My speech was slurred.

"You didn't pick us up, and Dad didn't answer his phone, so Coach took us home. We saw your car in the driveway, and Ms. Hyman next door told us you left in an ambulance," Morgan said.

I turned my head back to the man in the corner. This time I made out Corey's face. "Corey..." was all I managed to say before I burst into tears.

I heard him move and then felt his hand on my shoulder. "It's alright, Mona-Lisa," he said softly.

I hated to cry in front of my kids. I hated to cry, period. Nevertheless, I cried, because there was so much to cry for. There was so much blood that I knew I must've lost the baby. Part of me wondered if I'd wished it away, and the other part of me knew better. I cried because I'd made a mess of my life. I cried because I'd dragged my sons into that mess. I cried because I loved Corey. I cried because I'd lost Corey.

My tears finally ended, and I tried to smile at the boys. "I'm ok," I lied.

Blair nodded. Morgan wiped tears from his own face. "Mama, I'm sorry," Morgan said. He bent over and hugged me tightly.

"Hey, why don't you guys see what you can find in the snack bar? My treat," Corey said.

The boys looked at me for approval. I smiled weakly and said, "Go on."

Corey handed them some money, and I watched them slowly leave my hospital room.

"The doctor said you lost a lot of blood, and you'll have to stay here overnight," Corey said. There was worry in his eyes.

I nodded. "The baby?"

"The baby's fine. He said the placenta is in the wrong place or something. You'll have to take it easy from now on."

"Oh, thank God." I was surprised at how relieved I was. But I guess that no matter how I felt about Wasif, the baby was still mine, and I loved him or her nonetheless.

He placed his hand gently on my stomach. "So this is what you meant by your circumstances changing? Why didn't you just tell me?" he said softly.

A tear rolled down my cheek as I nodded again. "I'm so sorry, Corey. I'm so ashamed of myself. I love you. I really do. I wasn't trying to get pregnant, but when I realized that I was, I knew I had to stay with Wasif. It's not your responsibility. It's Wasif's."

He leaned close to my face. "Mona, I love you. *I love you.* A baby isn't gonna change that. I would do anything for you. I told you. I want a family. Now it'll just be bigger." The tears came again. This time, Corey wrapped his arms around me.

"I thought you hated me," I whimpered into his neck.

"I could never hate you, baby. I love you with all my heart."

He held me for a long while and then said, "I almost lost you for good today. I'm not taking any more chances. You're coming home with me in the morning so that I can take care of you. We'll figure out the rest later."

I nodded. There was no place I'd have rather been than with Corey Sanders, no matter the consequences. "Corey. I need to tell you something. It's important."

"Ok, tell me," he said into my ear.

"Ok, please don't be angry with me. It's about the boys..."

◆◆◆

Three days passed before Wasif came looking for me at Corey's apartment. Thankfully, Corey had gone back to work, and the boys were at school. I needed to talk to Wasif alone.

I opened the door and let him in without a word. I sat down on the sofa, and Wasif sat in an easy chair across from me. He looked tired, like he hadn't had much sleep. "How are you feeling?" he asked.

"Better."

Wasif clasped his hands in his lap and stared down at them. "My dad told me he spoke with you. Did he upset you? Is that why you ended up in the hospital, because if it is, I'll never forgive—"

I shook my head. "No. It had nothing to do with that. He actually didn't upset me all that much. It's placenta previa or at least that's what the doctor says."

He nodded and looked me in the eye. "The baby's ok?"

"Yes."

"Good. I tried to see you at the hospital, but your big boyfriend was guarding the door like a pit bull."

I frowned. "I didn't see you there."

"Right after he threatened to kick my butt, he told me you were asleep."

I shrugged. "Oh, then I probably was."

"Mo, I've come to take you home."

I shook my head. "I'm not going, Wasif. I can't keep pretending. I can't do this anymore. It's over."

I could see tears in his eyes. "Please, Mo. I love you. I love you *so much*. You've got to know that. Fifteen years. *Fifteen years* of history and you wanna just throw it away? I've left my wife for you. We can get a new house, a new car, whatever you want. Just don't leave me. "

I closed my eyes and sighed. "Wasif, you didn't leave your wife for me. You did that for yourself. If you'd been thinking about me, you never would have married her in the first place. We'd been together four years before you even married her. You should've stood up to your father, but you didn't. No, it was never me you were thinking about."

"I'm sorry. *I'm so sorry.* What do you want me to say or do to make it up to you? I need you, Mo. You know that. Please stop this and come home with me."

I shook my head and dropped my eyes to the floor.

"So what are you going to do? Live in this old factory with Sanders? Am I supposed to let another man raise my kids? I can't do that, Mo."

"Wasif, you can still help raise our kids. Honestly, you were never a full-time father anyway."

"I did my best."

"And you can still do your best. You can be as active as you want to be in our children's lives. You don't have to be sleeping with me in order to be their father."

"You're more than that to me, and you know it. I want you to be my wife now."

"Maybe it's just too little too late, Wasif. All I know is that we want different things in life now."

A single tear rolled down Wasif's cheek. "Mo, I love you. I always have. If I've ever done anything to hurt you, I apologize. I never ever meant to hurt you. I really tried to take care of you and the boys."

I reached over and grasped his hand. "Wasif, I'm not saying that you're not a man of your word. I'm not disputing that you've taken care of us. I appreciate all you've done. But let's not act like I didn't make any sacrifices. You married that woman because you felt like you had to. I went along with it, and I never complained. Being with Corey is what I have to do, what I *want* to do. All I'm asking is that you respect that. You don't have to like it or even agree with it. Just respect it and let me go."

Wasif hung his head. "I don't know where to go from here. What am I supposed to do now? You've been a part of my life for so long."

"I can't tell you what to do. If you love your wife at all, then try to save your marriage. I just know that this has to end."

He nodded then looked me in the eye. "If this doesn't work out with you and Sanders, there's no coming back. I'll always take care of my children, but if it's over between us, then it's over for good."

"I agree wholeheartedly."

"Have you told the boys?"

I shook my head. "Not yet. I think we should tell them together. Wasif, I need to tell you something, and it will probably upset you."

"Well, I don't see what you can say that would upset me any further."

"Um, I don't think that Morgan is your son."

He stared at me but didn't reply. I figured that he was either too shocked or too mad to speak, so I went on. "I didn't realize it until recently. It was hard to tell. I mean, my mother's of mixed race and Morgan has so many of my features, I just figured he'd taken more after my side than yours. I actually didn't even realize that it was possible for fraternal twins to have two different fathers. That's what I was researching on the computer that day. Blair is yours, I'm certain of that. But I'm almost positive that Morgan is Corey's son."

He nodded slowly. "I already knew that."

I frowned. "W…what?"

"I figured it out years ago. I just didn't care. Have you told them?"

I was in shock. "N…no."

"Does Corey know?"

"Yes. I told him a couple of days ago. I thought that the three of us could tell them together."

"Ok."

"Wasif, if you knew, why didn't you say anything?"

"Like I said, I didn't care. I loved them. I loved you. That's all that mattered to me."

"But, Corey deserved to know. He's missed out on most of Morgan's life."

"Just like I'll miss out on my new baby's life?"

"No, you won't. I'd never keep him or her from you. You know that."

"I hope you're telling the truth, Mo."

"Of course I am."

He nodded. "I want Morgan to know that he'll always be my son as far as I'm concerned."

"Ok."

He stood to leave, and I walked him to the door. He turned to me with sad eyes. "For the record, I really love you, Mo. I always have. I always will."

I kissed him softly on the lips. "I know you love me. I thank you for all you've done for me and for being such a good father to my sons." I hugged him and then closed the door behind him.

Chapter 23

"Same Ole Love"

He's a handsome little fella'. I think he looks like you," Corey said as he leaned over and kissed my cheek.

I smiled up him. He was a beautiful baby, but Corey was lying about him looking like me. I could already tell that he was just like Wasif. "Thank you, Corey."

He sat down in the chair next to the bed. "You still going with the name Wasif picked out?"

"Yeah, I guess it's only fair since I named Blair and Morgan. Besides, Sahib is a nice name."

"Yeah, I guess it is. What's it mean?" Corey asked.

"Master."

I looked up to see that it was Wasif who'd joined our conversation.

"That's nice," I said.

He walked to the foot of the bed and nodded towards

Corey. "How you doing?"

Corey nodded. "What's up, man?"

Wasif walked around to the side of the bed. "Can I hold him?"

I smiled up at him and nodded. I handed the baby to him, and he took him into his arms and moved across the room to the window. He smiled down at him and rubbed his cheek with his fingertip. Corey never took his eyes off of Wasif.

I reached over and held Corey's hand. He smiled at me as he rubbed his thumb across my wedding band.

Wasif kissed the baby's cheek and whispered something to him in Punjabi, then walked over to the bed and handed him back to me. "Another boy. I'm so proud. He's beautiful. Thank you for letting me see him."

"Anytime," I said.

"You ok? You need anything?" Wasif asked.

"Everything's been taken care of," Corey said as he twisted his own wedding band around on his finger.

Wasif looked at Corey for a moment and then said, "Yeah, ok. Where are Blair and Morgan?"

"Downstairs. In the cafeteria," Corey said.

"I'll run by and see them before I get back to work, then. I'm gonna head to the nurses' station right now and sign those papers so that Sahib will have my last name. Talk to you later, Mo." Wasif nodded at Corey and then left the room.

Corey relaxed his posture, and I wondered if things would ever get better between the two of them. Then again, I guess I should be glad they were getting along as well as they were. At least the heated arguments and mutual death threats had ended. And thankfully, none of that had gone down in front of the boys.

"Corey, do you want to hold him?" I asked.

His eyes lit up. "Can I?"

"Of course, he's yours, too. And don't think that I'mma be getting up in the middle of the night by myself."

Corey laughed as he took him into his arms. "I wouldn't let you do that." He sat back down in the chair and cradled him as he kissed his forehead. Sahib looked like a little doll in Corey's huge arms. Blair and Morgan came into the room and stood next to Corey to get a look at their brother. DNA tests had proven my suspicions correct. They'd taken the news about Corey being Morgan's dad better than I'd thought, but they were still adjusting to the changes in their lives. We all were. No more credit card shopping sprees for me, but then again, I didn't really miss that stuff at all. Things weren't perfect, but I had love, and I had a real family.

I smiled and said, "I think you finally got your family, Coach Sanders."

Corey looked up the boys and then at me. "I did, didn't I?"

Epilogue

I stood in the doorway, with Sahib on my hip, and watched as Corey and the boys left for school. I waved goodbye to them and ducked back inside the house in time to answer my ringing cell phone. "Hello?"

"Um, is this Mona-Lisa Dandridge?" It was a female voice on the other end.

"Yes, who's calling?"

"This is Gina Grant. You called me awhile back, asking about your sister..."

For more information on missing children, go to:

www.missingkids.com

For more information about child abuse:

http://childwelfare.gov/can

For more information on bullying, go to:

stopbullyingnow.hrsa.gov

For information about the author, go to:

adriennethompsonwrites.webs.com

Excerpt from

When You've Been Blessed

(Feels Like Heaven)

Available Spring 2012

I lay asleep, secure in my husband's arms, when his cell phone rang. By then, I was used to late night calls from church members reporting that a loved one was sick or had entered the hospital or had passed away. I even kept an outfit hanging in the closet in case Apollo and I had to make an unexpected trip in the middle of the night. But the calls usually came to the house phone. Only church officials or family members had his cell number. I lifted my head up from his chest and shook his shoulder.

"Apollo, your phone's ringing," I said.

"Hmm?" he responded groggily.

"Honey, your phone's ringing. You want me to get it?"

He shook his head and rubbed his eyes. "No, I'll get it. No sense in both of us having to break our rest."

My rest is already broken, I thought.

Apollo kissed my forehead then sat up on the side of the bed and pulled on his boxers and a t-shirt as he answered the phone.

"Hello?" he said. He listened to the caller for a moment and then said, "Alright, hold on a minute."

He stood and left the room. I lay back down and closed my eyes but found it impossible to fall back to sleep. My mind was reeling, wondering who was on the phone and what had happened. Finally, I sat up on the side of the bed and wrapped my robe around the fleshy curves of my body. I ran my hand through the soft twists on my head and slid my feet into my slippers.

I headed out of the room, having decided to get a glass of water from the kitchen. I walked down the hall towards the winding staircase and as I passed our son AJ's room, noticed that his light was on. *I guess he finally made it home.* I peeped through the slightly open door and saw that is was Apollo, not AJ, who was in the room. Apollo was sitting on the side of AJ's bed with his back to the door having a rather hushed conversation on the phone. I stood there for a moment and then told myself not to eavesdrop. *He'll tell me about it when he hangs up. He always does.*

I continued to the kitchen, fixed a glass of water, and headed back up the stairs. This time when I passed by AJ's room, I could hear Apollo raising his voice. I stopped by the door and listened.

"Don't you ever call me at this time of night again, you understand? And you sure as hell better not come to my house. We'll deal with this later," he said in a harsh whisper.

I raised my eyebrows and wondered who he was talking to and what he was talking about. I stood there for a few more seconds, but he lowered his voice and I couldn't make out what he was saying.

Not wanting to get caught eavesdropping, I headed to the bedroom and settled back into the bed. A few minutes later, Apollo returned to our bedroom, climbed into the bed, and spooned himself behind me.

"Who was that?" I asked.

"Nobody... one of the deacons about some program. Go back to sleep, baby."

I frowned. "A deacon at this time of night? Which deacon?"

"Yeah, I'm gonna have a talk with him in the morning." He only half answered my question.

He snuggled closer to me and kissed my shoulder. I opened my mouth to reply but then decided against it. I was pretty positive that Apollo was lying, but I didn't want to argue. We never argued, and I liked it that way. I closed my eyes and tried to sleep, but couldn't. That phone call and what I'd heard Apollo saying to the caller was all I could think of. I lay there wide awake for what felt like hours listening to Apollo's breathing and finally, having waited as long as I could, slipped out of the bed and quietly walked around it and picked Apollo's phone up from the night table.

I tipped out into the hallway. I shook my head and thought, *Lord, I can't believe I'm checking his phone. We've been married for twenty years, and I'm checking his phone like some kind of jealous crazy person.*

"I'm not doing this," I whispered to myself.

I turned back towards our bedroom door but couldn't make myself move. *Okay, I'll just check it and see that it was one of the deacons like he said, and then I can get some sleep.* I took a deep breath and then clicked the button on Apollo's phone until his call log popped up. The last call received did not have a name programmed with it but for some reason, it looked familiar to me. I stood there for a moment and then it dawned on me where I'd seen the number. I quickly walked down the stairs and into the living room. I picked up a piece of paper from the coffee table. On it I'd written Lisa Donley's number. I closed my eyes and then held the paper up next to the phone. Just as I'd suspected, the numbers were the same.

Why was Lisa calling him in the middle of the night? Better yet, what was she doing with his personal cell number? And why had Apollo lied about who was on the phone? I stood there for a minute or so and tried to decide whether or not I should confront Apollo about the phone call. As it turned out, I didn't have to. As I stood there contemplating my next move, Apollo's voice shocked me out of my thoughts.

"What are you doing down here? I missed you," he asked in his booming baritone voice.

I spun around, still holding his phone in my hand. I stood there and stared at him, but did not answer his question.

"And what are you doing with my phone?" he added with a frown.

"What were you doing on the phone with that girl?" I countered.

"What? Who? You been checking my phone, Tonya?" Apollo said, raising his voice a little.

"Answer the question, Apollo. You know what girl I'm talking about. I know this is her number because she gave it to me when she was here."

He shook his head. "I can't believe that after twenty years of marriage you are actually checking up on me. Come on, Tonya. This is ridiculous."

I shut my eyes tightly. "Well, you put me in this position. Why did you lie about who was on the phone? How did that girl get your number?"

"Tonya, is this for real? You think I got something going on with that girl? You know better than that. Come on and let's go back to bed." He reached for my arm and I snatched away from him.

"Apollo, you haven't answered one question. Why did you lie?!"

"Okay, okay. She got my number from her mother. She needed to talk about her trouble, so I talked to her. That's all."

"Then why did you tell her not to call you or come by here?"

"I never said any such thing."

He was lying. I couldn't believe that he was standing there looking me straight in the eye and lying! He'd never lied to me before, had he?

"Oh my G—you're lying! You said it. *I heard you*, Apollo."

"What?! Now you're eavesdropping on my conversations? What's gotten into you?"

I folded my arms across my chest. "Maybe the better question is, 'Who've *you* gotten in to?' Are you her baby's father?"

He laughed. "What?! Are you serious? Didn't we just make love a few hours ago? Did that feel like I've been with someone else?"

I dropped my eyes. Apollo's lovemaking always made me feel like I was the only woman he wanted, like he'd bottled up all of his passion and only released it when I returned home. Even after twenty years, he couldn't seem to get enough of me.

"Did it?" he repeated.

I shifted my weight on my feet and looked up at Apollo. "Well, no, but why lie? You've never lied to me before."

Apollo moved closer to me and placed his hands on my shoulders. "She asked me to keep it confidential. She told me who the father was, and I knew if I told you she'd talked to me, you'd want to know what we talked about. I was just trying to respect her privacy," he said softly.

I shook my head and sighed. "I'm sorry. I don't know what's going on with me. I guess I'm out on the road so much, I just worry about things between us sometimes."

He smiled down at me and kissed me softly, sending a spark through me. It was amazing that he still had such an effect on me. "I love you, baby. There's no one else I want in this world. Now come on back to bed. We got church in the morning."

I nodded. "Okay."

As we began to walk back to our bedroom, Apollo's phone rang again. I had forgotten that I was still holding it. I looked at it for a moment and then handed it to him. He looked at the screen and frowned.

"I don't know this number," he said. He pressed the button, accepted the call, and cautiously said, "Hello?"

I watched as he listened attentively to the voice on the other end. His eyes widened as he nodded and repeatedly said, "Okay." Finally, he hung up and turned to me. "Well, it seems that our son is in jail."

I gasped. "WHAT?! What happened? Is he okay?"

"The officer said something about an assault and battery charge. I'll get dressed and go bail him out."

"O...okay. You want me to come?"

"No, stay here. I'll be back with him as soon as I can."

"Okay."

Ten minutes later, Apollo left for the police station and I sat in the living room with my Bible open. After reading a few scriptures, I knelt down in front of the sofa and began to pray for my family...

Lovely Blues- Bluesday Book II
(Special Sneak Peak)

I sat in our living room, staring at the blank page of the notebook that lay in my lap. I was due back in the studio in a couple of weeks and I really needed to be writing. But I couldn't. Well, actually I could, but I just didn't feel like doing much of anything. I had no energy and I had to fight to climb out of bed in the morning. Truthfully, I would've been happy to sleep the day away.

Or to drink.

There, I said it. I wanted to drink. I wanted to drive to the liquor store and buy a big tall bottle of something and drink it all in one sitting. I wanted to feel drunk and numb. The desire was so strong that I hadn't left my house in days, afraid I'd give in to temptation. I had my AA sponsor on speed dial and don't think I hadn't been harassing her. Her name was Patsy and she was more than patient and kind with me, but I was beginning to feel like I was imposing on her. After all, she had her own life and her own problems to deal with.

I shifted my eyes from the notebook to my keys on the coffee table to the wedding portrait that hung over the mantle. I missed

Reggie. We lived in the same house and slept in the same bed, but I still missed him. I felt my eyes well up. I shook my head. *No crying.* Crying and whining and letting things happen to me had gotten me nowhere in the past. I stood from the sofa and grabbed my keys. *I'm gonna fix this right now.*

I weaved through the traffic, past the liquors stores, I might add, and made my way to TSU. I walked into that building, threw my hand up at the department secretary, and headed straight to Reggie's office where I flung the door open without bothering to knock. There was a student in his office and no doubt they were having a meeting, but I didn't care. When I entered the office, the smile Reggie had been wearing faded. That stung, but I didn't let it deter me.

"Um, Bobbie, what's wrong?" he asked as if he didn't know.

Ignoring the question, I extended my hand towards the young man sitting opposite Reggie's desk and smiled. "I'm Coach Darrough's wife."

The young man returned my smile and nodded. "Yes, ma'am. I'm Greg Larson."

"Pleased to meet you, Greg. I need to speak with my husband for a moment. Do you mind?"

The young man shook his head and then stood to leave. "Oh, no, ma'am. See you later, Coach," he said.

I closed and locked the door behind him and then took the seat the young man had vacated.

"Bobbie, what's going on? How you just gonna come in here and take over?" Reggie asked, sounding annoyed.

"I'm here because as hard you are running from me, that's how hard I'm willing to chase you."

Made in the USA
Lexington, KY
09 October 2012